CHALLENGES

A Trip To Remember

David Rigby

Nightengale Press
A Nightengale Media LLC Company

CHALLENGES

For information about Nightengale Press please
visit our website at www.nightengalepress.com.
Email: publisher@nightengalepress.biz
or send a letter to:
Nightengale Press
10936 N. Port Washington Road. Suite 206
Mequon, WI 53092
Library of Congress Cataloging-in-Publication Data

Rigby, David,
Challenges/ David Rigby
ISBN:1-933449-36-5
Non-Fiction/Canoeing

First Published by Nightengale Press in the USA

October 2006

10 9 8 7 6 5 4 3 2 1

Printed at
Lightning Source Inc.
1246 Heil Quaker Boulevard
La Vergne, Tennessee 37086

Challenges

8/8/04 Sunday

Getting There!

"Back paddle! Get away from that tree!" I bellowed.

It was too late. Alexis and Kellie screamed while thrusting their paddles in front of their faces to protect themselves from the jagged branches of the fallen tree. In horror we watched as the doomed canoe rammed the half submerged tree, slowly pitched to the upstream side, and began to fill with water. The two hapless girls were thrown into the swirling currents of the river; their faces contorted in terror. Screams were quickly silenced as the struggling students were dragged beneath the surface and into the mass of tangled branches.

I bolted upright in my bed. Another dream! Thank God! I glanced at my clock which read 3:00 A.M. There were still two long hours before my alarm would go off. Would this night ever end?

My outstretched hand found and shut off the alarm almost before it started to ring. Sleep had not been good.

The night had been spent tossing and turning while worrying about all the things that could go wrong on the trip. At 1:00 A.M. I had crawled out of bed and stumbled out to the garage to check that the tent poles were packed. Cold cement chilled my bare feet, but the poles were found right in the tent bag where they belonged. At 3:00 A.M. I had dreamt about Kellie and Alexis drowning. Could Kellie handle the river? Did we have enough chaperones? Would the weather cooperate? Would the vehicles break down? Would the new packs work? In the darkness of pre-dawn, I checked all the food packs for the third time. My stomach twisted and growled with anguish.

On this bright sunny August morning, I was questioning everything. Why, at the age of fifty-three, had I decided to take ten 7th grade students on a five day wilderness canoe trip? Sure, I had done it before; in fact, I have done this same trip for the past thirty years. But each year at the beginning of another trip it was the same. The responsibility is so great; everyone is so trusting. I allowed myself to wallow in self doubt and worry. "Why do I do this?" I questioned.

Knowing it would be a week before I showered again; I relished the warm flowing water. Then a hot cup of coffee helped shake the cob webs from my head and clear my thoughts. Showered, dressed, and my normal morning routine complete; the phone rang. It was 6:00 A.M.

"Victoria can't get her air mattress to fit in her pack. Can she bring another pack along also?" an anxious mother questioned.

"I'm sorry, but no. If anything doesn't fit into the pack, then it has to be left behind."

Hanging up the phone, I shook my head and smiled realizing that it is always the same. Parents, especially moms, worry so much and want to be so helpful, but most just don't have a clue concerning packing for wilderness travel. Every year at least one student will have his or her loving mom carefully pack each pair of underwear and each item of clothing in separate plastic bags. Usually about the second day we will hear that exasperated student shouting from their tent, "I hate plastic bags! I hate plastic bags!"

Several years ago I had received a phone call late on the Saturday night before the trip.

"I was in the Navy for 25 years, and I know how to pack. This stuff will not fit in my son's duffel!" blasted a frustrated father without so much as a hi or hello.

"Sir," I started quietly and patiently, "I am sorry, but I have never been in the Navy. However, I have been doing this trip for nearly thirty years, and I am using the same type pack as your son. My gear is packed and sitting next to the front door with space to spare. It does fit; I'll see you in the morning." I hung up.

Victoria would show up with an extra pack, and I would have to explain again how the canoes could only hold so much gear and that loose extra packs just could not be tolerated. That is just the way it always was!

Sleepy students started to arrive around 7:00 A.M. Their parents wanted to help.

"I'll tie down the canoes," a dad volunteered.

"I'll check the trailer lights!" chipped in another.

"Where do I put my daughter's pack?"

I turned around and saw two Moms in my garage busily trying to re-pack their daughters' packs.

"Whoa!" my voice cut through the quiet morning. Holding my arms above my head, I laughed while announcing, "Parents, this is not your trip! You are not going! Say your good-byes. I don't mean to be rude, but please leave!"

Sheepishly, dads came down from the trailer, moms stopped packing, and good-byes were said. By 7:30 all was packed and we were on our way.

The ten hour ride passed quickly. We had an unusual mixture of only two boys and eight girls. All were twelve or thirteen years old, just having finished 7th grade. The boys were good talkers, and the girls had fun with travel games invented to help make time pass more quickly. By 5:30 P.M. we pulled into the parking lot of Jadwin Canoe Rental. For the past twenty years, the owner, Darrel Blackwell, has handled the shuttle for our vehicles. With final shuttle arrangements made, we turned off the main highway and started along the steep road leading down into the river valley.

The blacktop ended and was replaced by rutted gravel surrounded by dense oak–hickory forest. Our caravan began a steep descent into the valley of the scenic national waterway. Situated at the very bottom of the deep river-carved basin was the location of the launch site for our fifty-six mile paddle trip. Two bridges, no towns, and miles of rugged forest lay ahead. Caves were waiting to be explored, sheer cliffs were beckoning to be climbed, and spring fed waters danced over ancient rocks. The river awaited our group's arrival.

Anticipation was rising, and I reacted by pushing down harder on the accelerator. Our kayak-laden truck bounced and lurched over the rugged gravel until it swept around the final turn. The two students riding with me were on the edge of their seats, almost holding their breath. I grasped the stirring wheel in a white knuckled strangle hold. The truck burst out from under the shade of the trees and out into the bright sun. The river surged serenely before us.

Put-In

There she was, like an old friend, the river seemed to welcome me upon my return. Her spring-fed, frigid waters sparkled and danced in the bright sunlight. The twisted anguish I had been feeling in my gut disappeared, and a broad smile crept across my face. I pulled my foot gently up and off of the accelerator and allowed the truck to glide slowly over the low water bridge. The road narrowed to one lane and ran over a cement dam. The river on the upstream side was wide and pristine. The water level was less than a foot below the road. A good rain storm would make this thoroughfare treacherous and impassable. The dam had nine metal culverts protruding from the down river side. Water shot wildly from these pipes, and the river swept rapidly off into the thick woodlands and dolomite cliffs below.

Our caravan crossed the low water bridge slowly and turned onto a wide gravel bar. The river at the put-in point was just over twenty feet wide, only a couple of feet deep, and was ripping through the wooded banks at a ferocious pace. Two old aluminum Grumman canoes and two new bright red plastic Old Town canoes were unloaded from the canoe trailer and gently placed in a shallow eddy at the water's edge. Three 14.5 foot Perception Carolina sea kayaks were placed just downstream from the canoes.

Each student and chaperone had their own water proof Bill's bag. These are similar to an army duffel bag except that they are equipped with padded shoulder straps and a convenient suitcase-like grip. Red, blue, green, and yellow; the never-used-before packs sparkled unblemished. That would soon change.

Two yellow York packs, which are large plastic boxes 24″ tall, 18″wide and 30″ long, held the cook gear and water testing equipment. Food was packed into two small coolers and water in two large jugs.

Lindsey and Kailee were in my canoe. Diane (Ms. Dorn) has Abby and Caity in her old Grumman. Kellie has volunteered to stern the student canoe in which a reluctant Alexis is paddling the bow. They are using one of the bright red Old Town canoes. Tina (Mrs. Partridge) guides the two kayakers, Victoria and Kate. Chris (Mr. Setzler) will bring up the rear with Ricky and Bill in the other Old Town.

Three Bill's Bags and one equipment pack needed to be carried in each canoe. "Wow, this is freezing!" screeched Kailee when she walked into the cold water.

"Grab the bow," I ordered, and the girls held the front of the canoe while standing knee deep in the racing water. Their feet sank into the gravel bottom and pebbles found their way into their shoes. They held on tight, trying to keep their balance while I began to load our gear.

My Bill's Bag was placed in the stern compartment of our old Grumman canoe. There are four areas that can be used for gear in these canoes. The stern compartment is in the back and the bow compartment the front. In between there are two empty areas referred to as the stern and bow duff sites.

"Let me help you, Mr. Rigby!" offered Kailee as she splashed to shore.

We hoisted the heavy York pack containing river testing gear, which included a $500.00 microscope and a $300.00 underwater camera, and placed it in the stern duff area along with Kailee's Bill's Bag. Lindsey's bag was put in the bow duff and would be used as a back rest for Kailee. Fishing poles were placed under the side ridges called the gunnels. The canoe now sank so low in the water that the gunnels were just inches above the surface.

Chris Setzler, another science teacher and chaperone, gave a quick talk about river safety. Chris, now in his thirties, had been one of my students years ago. This was his tenth year teaching science alongside me, and his tenth canoe trip. Being a track coach and long distance runner, he takes pride in his physical condition, and his well muscled physique shows it. He is also an organizational freak.

"Look out for strainers, don't bunch up, and if you hit a rock, don't lean upstream," he lectured to the anxious students. Lindsey was seated in the bow with her paddle ready and dipped in the water. Kailee had plopped into the bow duff and had her paddle shoved into the gravel bottom. Both were tense and anxious.

I don't sit on the seat, but use the stern plate. I developed this habit while guiding Canadian canoe trips back in the 70's. My wide brimmed cowboy hat was tilted low over my brow to keep the sun out of my eyes. My sandal-clad feet rested in the water on either side of the canoe keeping the craft steady despite the tug of the flowing water. I could not help but smile while listening to Chris. "Couldn't have said it better myself," I thought. It was time to start.

I lifted my feet, but the canoe did not budge. "Out you guys!" I declared to my young canoe mates. They scramble out, squealed as their feet contacted the water, and then tugged at the heavy canoe. With metal scraping against rock, the three of us pushed and pulled the boat out into the current until it was floating freely. I held the stern while Lindsey tried to get back into the canoe.

"Don't get water in the canoe!" Kailee yelled at Lindsey.

Lindsey held up her foot high above the water, let it drain, and than placed it over the gunnel and into the canoe. Loose gravel shifted under her other foot while fast powerful currents ripped at her leg. She lost her balance and plopped straight down into the frigid water. Seated in the water, Lindsey had one foot draped up and over the gunnel inside of the canoe. Uttering a forlorn groan, she dolefully struggled to get back to her feet. Kailee and I could not contain ourselves. We laughed so hard that we almost joined Lindsey in the water. Finally, both Lindsey and Kailee were back in the boat and ready to paddle.

"In about three bends, there is a spot where we really need to be careful. There is a tree in the river that has tipped and trapped many a canoe. It is wicked," I warned the whole group.

Back on the stern plate, I lifted my feet and placed them into the boat. Quietly, reverently, and unnoticed by the others, I gave the river a fisted salute. "Good to be back," I whispered. The strong current quickly propelled the canoe towards the first bend.

First Paddle

Four heavily loaded canoes and three kayaks sped downriver through the densely wooded, cliff-strewn Ozark wilderness. Diane Dorn was the chaperone paddling stern in the second canoe. Her long braided hair was tucked neatly under a beat up old leather cowboy hat. She followed my canoe, avoiding as many rocks as possible. Her vast outdoor experience included a solo trip to the Artic, a trout study in Russia, and traveling across Greenland. She possesses a dry sense of humor and a near sadistic pleasure for hard work. Her two young female canoe mates had no idea what was in store for them.

Abby sat low in the bow duff, her big brown eyes absorbing everything. Shy, she seldom speaks but has the reputation of being one of the most sincere, polite girls in the school. Caity sits tall on the bow seat, her red hair flaring in the wind. She wears a constant smile on her face and is always ready with a loud contagious laugh.

Kellie and Alexis are both strong girls with long blond hair. Kellie is confident in the stern, but Alexis is nervous. She would much rather be in a canoe with a chaperone. Kellie is doing well and followed Diane's canoe down the rock-strewn river.

The kayakers are led by Tina, (Mrs. Partridge.) She has an overwhelming amount of energy and is a tireless worker. This is her second river trip with Chris and me. Being the mother of three children, she exudes a feeling of compassion that all the students relish.

Kate and Victoria paddle the other two kayaks. Introduced to kayaking earlier this year, Kate has fallen in love with the sport and confidently guides her boat with powerful strokes. Her quiet, subdued personality contrasts with the brilliant sparkle of excitement emanating from her eyes. It is clear she is savoring every detail of this adventure. Victoria has shoulder length dark brown hair and large brown eyes. She nervously chatters and laughs while trying to keep up with Tina and Kate.

Chris sits low in his canoe helping Kellie with a constant flow of positive reinforcement. Bill and Ricky are with him and are the only two boys on this female-dominated trip. Bill is a blonde haired, blue eyed, walking encyclopedia who, while paddling in the bow, expounds little-known facts about anything and everything. He displays sincere compassion for others and is always a willing helper. Ricky instantly finds his niche in the duff seat. His long brown hair is always getting in his eyes. Quiet and soft spoken, he is a sincere young teen and a quick learner. Our heavily loaded flotilla paddles around the first two bends and through several rocky shoots without mishap.

"Rock!" yelled Lindsey. "Rock on the right! Rock in front! Rock on the left! Oh no, a log! We just went over a log! More rocks coming! Rocks everywhere!"

Lindsey nervously screamed out the location of rocks and logs in every direction while Kailee sits in her duff seat giggling and laughing at her panicky partner.

The loud raspy screech of metal scraping rock tore through the quiet of the river basin. We did scrape bottom a lot, but in the shallow quick water of the upland portion of the river, it could not be helped.

"It's because of my big fat butt!" I declared loudly just after we scraped particularly hard on a rocky ledge.

A sudden loud scrape from behind our canoe caused me to turn and look back upstream. Diane's canoe was lodged solidly on the same rock we had just hit. Without saying a word, her eyes glared a clear message. "You make one comment about my butt and you're dead!" (Silently I paddled ahead. I'm no fool.)

The current ahead swung strongly to the right, directly at a massive rock ledge on the outside bank. About eight feet to the ledge's inside was a large white wave which indicated the presence of a submerged log. Shallow gravel made the inside of the turn impassible. We were approaching our first treacherous section of river, the section that had swamped, held, and even destroyed many canoes in the past.

"Follow me, but don't bunch up," I instructed the group. "When I tell you, draw hard on the left." I instructed a very quiet Lindsey, "Let's do it!"

We approached cautiously; our heavily loaded canoe was about as easy to handle as a pregnant elephant. I pointed the bow directly at the swirling white wave and dug my paddle into the water hard.

"Draw!"

Lindsey reached her paddle far out to the left of the canoe, stuck her paddle blade into the water, and pulled with all her strength back towards the canoe. I reached to the right and did the same. Our canoe pivoted left and shot past the submerged log. One hard pry stroke, the opposite of a draw, and our canoe straightened and shot out into a calm pool.

"Yeah!" paddles held overhead, Lindsey and Kailee cheered in unison.

Tina, Victoria, and Kate drove their kayaks through the shoot, each separately following the same run I had made. They joined us in our deep quiet eddy, smiles spread from ear to ear.

Diane's canoe was next. There was no smile on Caity's face. Her paddle was out of the water resting uselessly across the gunnels, her eyes wide with fear. Abby was so low in the canoe that she was almost invisible.

"Paddle, Caity! Paddle!" shouted Diane.

Caity sat frozen with fear. Diane drew hard and missed the submerged log, but could not recover and rammed the shore on the inside of the turn. At least they were safe.

Kellie and Alexis were next. They headed directly at the submerged log just as I had; only they did not turn.

Plowing directly on top the large wave, their canoe lurched violently! They both leaned exactly the way they needed, and just like experts, they countered the wave and shot into the pool by us.

"Back paddle, back paddle hard!" Chris yelled to his canoe partners.

They were following too close, and he had to steer his canoe to the outside of the turn to avoid Kellie and Alexis. With a loud thud, the stern of his canoe smacked into the rocky ledge, tilted, righted, and shot ahead to join us in our quiet eddy. Three of the four canoes had almost capsized, but the group was exuberant and vastly over confident.

"Piece of cake!"

"No problem!"

"That was fun!"

I shook my head and turned my canoe downstream and continued to paddle knowing we were lucky to have all made it through that section upright. At the end of the pool was a smooth gravel bar that we had used on many occasions as our first campsite. "Ready to camp?" I inquired.

"Let's keep going!"

"I'm having too much fun to stop yet!"

"Yeah, let's go on. We're not ready to stop!"

It was unanimous. We paddled on.

The sun had dipped below the high tree line of the steep cliffs. The dark green foliage of the trees began to take on a golden glow as the sun sank lower. The deep emerald green of the river glimmered like a ribbon of green, sparkling with thousands of diamonds.

Kailee turned to look at me with her big brown eyes sparkling, "This is so pretty," she almost whispered. "I never expected it to be so beautiful."

I nodded in agreement and paddled on silently. The only sounds were the gurgling of the river and an occasional cry from a disturbed Kingfisher.

After several miles of paddling in the dimming glow of a nearing sunset, a small white sand bar appeared on our river right. On the opposite side, a row of lichen and fern covered cliffs rose straight from the river. The current rocketed over submerged boulders and emptied into a deep pool at the base of a large open gravel bar. This would be our home for the night.

First Camp

Darkness was rapidly approaching. None of the students had ever camped liked this before, and everyone was tired from a long day. We had much to do, and everybody pitched in and began to work. First, the canoes had to be pulled up and emptied. Lindsey and Kailee struggled under the weight of their packs, but quickly they and the others had the boats emptied and the gear on the dry rocks of the gravel bar.

Second, we needed to get the tents up and gear stowed away. Chris and I discovered that spring floods had left the bar strewn with large jagged rocks. The smoothest area with the smallest rocks was right at the river's edge. These were the "softer" rocks. We decided to set up our tents in a row just feet from the water.

The eight girls shared two 4-person Eureka Timberline tents. Chris and I did the same. We had our tent up quickly and set about helping the students who had only seen these tents once before. Four tents were erected in a neat straight line. Ricky and Bill's smaller tent was first. Our tent was next, followed by two tents with four girls in each. Wet gear and packs were stored under tent flies between the tents and sleeping bags and gear set up inside. Diane had a one-person tent she set up off by herself and Tina always sleeps outside next to the fire.

Next, it was time to set up our kitchen. Chris took Bill and Ricky out to search for fire wood. I enlisted the help of Alexis and Kellie to carry my canoe up to a flat shelf-like ledge overlooking the river. I took the stern and Alexis and Kellie grabbed the bow. Together we easily carried the canoe up to the ledge and placed it gently on the rocks. Tina had found a large log. The four of us struggled under the weight but dragged the log over to the canoe. By turning the canoe up side down and placing the gunnels on the log, we created a flat table for our kitchen. Standing behind our new "table", I looked down at our neatly lined up tents at the river's edge. Upstream, a mist was beginning to develop on the flat water in the pool at the base of the lichen-covered cliffs.

"A kitchen with a view," I declared.

Diane had the other girls quietly, no, noisily turning the other canoes over and stowing paddles and life jackets neatly beneath them. The first camp is always the hardest. Students need to be directed for every detail. They have never done this before, so they need patient direction to get jobs accomplished. As chaperones, we don't act as guides who do all of the work. Rather, we teach and instruct. It would probably be easier to just do it ourselves, but that is not our way.

"Look at all the crayfish!"

"Minnows are everywhere! Let's catch one!"

"Four skips on that rock."

In the early darkness of evening, the girls started to explore our rugged site. Two skipped rocks across the quiet pool. Others spread out along the shore checking out the swimming and crawling creatures. Lindsey even got out her air mattress and floated in the quick water. At the back of the camp, Chris and the boys returned dejectedly carrying a few small pieces of pathetic looking fire wood.

"I just can't find a honey hole!" Chris groaned, his shoulders slumping.

"Follow me!" I left my spot behind our upturned canoe and headed down the river bank. Chris and the boys quickly fell in line behind me, and we headed back into the woods along the shore. Thirty plus years of experience and "lots a luck" have always helped me find ample fire wood wherever I camp. Ignoring individual pieces of wood we headed far up the shore. Bill was at my side machine-gunning fact after fact of knowledge at me.

"Holy cripes, Bill, I should be writing this stuff down. I could be a millionaire if I wrote a book with all your information!" I wasn't kidding; the kid was amazing!

Then I saw it, a honey hole of fire wood. A downed tree with dead wood piled high around its base and along its main trunk spread out before us in the darkness. It probably was left as a remnant of the spring flooding, but I took my time and looked carefully for any unfriendly hosts. These wood piles are the perfect habitat for many different types of creatures including rattlesnakes. In the darkness I poked gently in amongst the tangled branches with a long dead stick. My stomach fluttered with excess adrenaline while I strained my senses looking for any type of motion. I hate snakes and did not want to encounter one here in the mass of tangled dead wood. Something brushed the back of my leg. I froze. Turning slowly so as not to move my leg, I twisted and stared down at the back of my foot. "Whew, just a stick!" Balanced precariously, I continued until finally I was satisfied our honey hole was safe.

I began breaking off pieces of wood and piling them in neat stacks which Chris, Bill, and Ricky carried back to the camp. It would be a cool night followed by a cold damp morning. A warm fire would be welcomed. Victoria,

Kailee, and most all the girls joined in the parade carrying the wood back to the site. Chris stayed back at camp and meticulously stacked and organized the wood into different piles depending on size. He even remembered to stash a good supply under our upturned canoe-table for breakfast.

Returning to camp with a small load myself, I helped Tina and Diane get out our supper of ham, cheese, turkey, bread, and shoe string potatoes. Students continued to explore, and they got themselves at least a bit acclimated to their new environment while we prepared a deli feast. Chris rounded up Ricky and Bill and patiently showed them how to build and light a campfire. Starting with a small piece of birch bark, he carefully placed small twigs in a neat teepee fashion. Slowly, they increased the size of the sticks and the teepee until he was satisfied. One match was all it took, and the flame began to work its way upward. Everything Chris does is neat and organized.

Soon a roaring fire was casting light on our kitchen table and supper. Students lined up in the darkness at the end of the canoe and made their way along its length selecting ingredients for their meal. Seated on my new camp stool, and using my trusty old Frisbee for a plate, I contently munched on my sandwich. Choosing a location just at the border of where the light of the fire met the darkness of the gravel bar, I tried to distance myself from the group so that I could observe.

Nervous anxiety prevailed throughout the group. Most had never even been camping, and now here they were six miles from a small road camped on a gravel bar in the middle of nowhere. No TV, no radios, no walk-men, no cell phones. They were all forced out of their normal comfort zones and thrust into something completely new and exciting. First nights are always chaotic. No one knows where anything is. No routines have been established. That will change! The students have been sitting most of the day. They have tons of excess energy. It was time for a challenge.

Chris and Diane organized the hike. Tina and all the students quickly grabbed their flash lights and were ready to head off. Just feet from the dimming fire, the world turned into total darkness. It was illuminated only by the thousands of stars in the sky and what appeared to be an equal amount of fire flies in the woods. Diane took control of the group and led them off into the darkness. Reaching the last flickering of light, she turned and gave me a nefarious grin.

First Night's Hike

It took all my self control not to burst out laughing. The students had no idea what was in store for them, and I had no idea how they would react or feel about this challenge. (It wasn't until after the trip, when I read their journals, that I could piece together that first night's hike.)

Kate's Journal

Ms. Dorn headed the hike. Tina was in the middle and Mr. Setzler at the end. I was up at the front with Ms. Dorn and Bill. Mr. Rigby stayed behind. After sitting in the cars all day and being in a totally new and different environment, we were all hyper and filled with energy. I really needed this hike and was glad we were finally going. The whole woods seemed to close in around us. It was so exciting! I had no idea where we were or where we were going.

The group noisily moved away from the fire. Flash light beams shot out in every direction resembling a London night in WWII with the spot lights searching desperately for the German bombers. Although our campsite was relatively flat, the terrain immediately beyond was extreme. We were at the base of a steep cliff with a rutted ATV trail being the only way to the top. Diane led the ascent up the steepest, most deeply rutted portion of the trail.

Bill's Journal

The sand trail led up a hill so slippery and steep that I had to put my flash light in my mouth and climbed on all fours. We left the openness of the river and continued into the dark woods.

The struggling group reached the top of the first climb only to find that there was a tall grassy clearing from which they could see a small ribbon of the river glistening quietly far below. Turning away from the river, they begin to move their way across the opening.

Bill's Journal

Once over the top, the trail seemed to go straight down into the earth and disappear. It was gone. We had hardly started and we had already lost any signs of a trail. We continued by walking in what we hoped was a straight line. We tried to follow the brilliant beams of our flashlights which reflected off the trees and danced up and into the starry night. Somehow we found a dirt road which branched in many directions. We only did rights. Each time we came to a T or a junction, we always chose the right. At least I think we did?

Diane has a great sense of direction and is a veteran wilderness hiker. She led the group across the trail-less clearing and found a series of maze-like ATV and four wheel drive roads. Any time they came to a junction, she always turned right. In this manner she led them further and further from the river and into the woods. She wanted the students to turn their flash lights off and walk in the darkness. She had no luck at this.

Kate's Journal

Most of us had new flashlights that were a riot. They had multiple color choices for us to select and use. Trudging noisily down the trail, we experimented with different colors. Red was the coolest, so we all turned to that color. Red beams flickered and flashed in every direction.

Whereas Diane has the keen ability to keep track of exactly where she is at all times, Chris and the others do not. Chris was busy looking for things to show the students and soon was successful.

Kate's Journal

Mr. Setzler stopped, and, using his normal dull flashlight as a pointer, showed us the biggest spider web I had ever seen. Its silken strands were spun between two large pine trees, and it glimmered ominously in the beam of his flashlight. I would hate to run into that web and didn't want to see its builder either. He also showed us what poison ivy looked like. My uncle had already shown me the three red stemmed leaves. He had also shown me how the leaves had a notch on one side. I had no problem recognizing it but wouldn't want to run into that either.

Diane was in her element and having a blast. She led the students up and down the steepest rut-filled trails she could find. The group moved further and further into the woods, struggling up hills, while slipping and sliding through mud filled trenches.

Bill's Journal

Sliding down a steep hill, I lost control and nearly fell into a large mud puddle. In the nick of time, I stopped and avoided getting soaked, but only momentarily. The girls behind me came skidding down the hill and plowed right into me. I lurched into the puddle, and my dry shoes were instantly filled with cold muddy water. At least I had remained upright!

We continued following Ms. Dorn along the edge of the puddles, and soon my wet feet were forgotten. For the first time in my life I saw the Milky Way. It stretched like a milky white cloud across the center of the sky, and it clearly stood out in the sparkling starry night.

Ms. Dorn ordered, "It's time to head back, but you guys are going to lead. Don't get us lost!"

"Thanks for the vote of confidence!" I thought to myself.

Back at camp I enjoyed the solitude. Night hikes used to be one of my favorites, but now my legs were too stiff and sore. Keeping the fire low, I got out my journal, the students' journals, and their writing utensils. In the dim flickering light of the fire, supplies were organized. I practiced reading from my journal while trying to formulate a strategy to stimulate the students to write. A barred owl called gently from across the river. I could just barely hear his low "Who Who Whoaaa" through the din of the multitude of screeching insects behind the camp. Time passed quickly while I sat writing. So much time passed that I began to wonder if Diane had led them too far or if something had happened.

Kailee's Journal

Kate and I were out in front leading the group. We were sure we were going the right way until Ms. Dorn started pointing out things that we hadn't noticed before. I started getting really nervous. Everything looked so different, yet it all looked the same. Were we going the right way? I really began to have doubts. We kept going and going, yet I just didn't know. We walked and walked until I got so tired I just wanted a car to pick me up and take me back to the campsite.

Chris wished he had paid more attention to where they had been going because he really was not sure if they were heading in the right direction. Tina had no clue and the students were all beginning to have their doubts. Diane was having a blast!

Bill's Journal

"Shhhh! Bill! Hold up!" whispered Ms. Dorn while tapping me gently on the shoulder. "Let's drop back and listen to the girls decide which way to go. I think they made a mistake."

"What's wrong?" from out of the darkness came Mr. Setzler's voice.

"We're going the wrong way!" Ms. Dorn repeated.

Everyone agreed that Ms. Dorn was wrong, so we continued on into the night.

The student-led group continued its aimless march through the dark Ozark woodlands. They quietly argued about which direction to go and slowly became more and more nervous. "Were they lost?" Was the question that began to creep into everyone's minds.

Bill's Journal

"I don't remember this field," whispered Kate.

"Me neither," Kailee replied dolefully.

"I told you soooo!" cooed a very confident Ms. Dorn. We let her take the lead

With Diane confidently in front, the group turned and back-tracked a short distance then quickly moved through the dark woods towards the river.

Bill's Journal

"Thank God!" I thought while we all openly rejoiced. We stood at the top of the hill that towered over our camp. The flickering light of Mr. Rigby's fire glowed softly in the trees below. Finally we knew where we were! Very much relieved, we crashed down the steep rocky slope to the fire.

With no quiet stealth what-so-ever, the young hoard was making their return. The quiet night silence was shattered by their tramping, laughing, and shouting. Diane had let them choose directions and had given them the freedom to make mistakes. They had done both and now joined me, sitting by the glimmering coals of the fire.

"We went forever!"

"Biggest spider web I ever saw!"

"My feet are soaked!"

"Awesome!"

When they settled down, they began staring at the red glowing coals of my fire, mesmerized by sudden flickers of flame. Quietly, I took out my journal. I had written it while on a month-long kayaking trip that past summer in California. With insect and river sounds murmuring in the surrounding trees, I read them the following segment about Jose, a woman who crossed paths with me in New Mexico.

6/7/04 (Rigby's Journal / Jose's Challenge)

I met my first real gypsy today, Josaline. I pulled into a rest area in New Mexico to get a map, and this drop-dead beautiful girl steps out in front of my truck. I can't help but notice her slender well muscled legs revealed under a loose fitting dress like my Gramma Eckert used to wear. Her long brown hair rested on her shoulders, and she flashed me a radiant smile. I waved her on, but she tossed her head, laughed and then waved me forward.

After parking, I walked into the center having to go to the bathroom desperately. To my chagrin they were cleaning, so

I had to wait 5 minutes. The lady behind the counter was helpful and had post cards, maps, and booklets for me. The beautiful dark-haired women heard where I was going, and having traveled to Santa Fe often, added some useful information. She introduced herself, Josaline, or Jose, was her name. The bathroom opened, so I quickly excused myself. She was gone when I came out. I took some coffee out to my truck and started looking at my new maps. Jose came out, waved, and came right over. She lives in her truck and sells coats at renaissance fairs. She was on her way to Colorado. I explained my plans, and she actually grabbed my shoulders and shook them with excitement.

She informed me that Clines Corner was a really unique spot and that she was going to stop there for a rest. Back in our separate vehicles, we left the rest area. I quickly passed her beat up truck with a mounted camper. Getting low in gas, I pulled in at Clines Corner. It was a pure tourist trap. I got out my chair and sat in the shade trying to figure out directions. Jose pulled up in her truck and I offered to buy her a cup of coffee. We talked for an hour with four cups of coffee apiece. She was a true gypsy, and it was clear she had led a fascinating life. For the past 18 years she has been "living with the earth" and had constantly been on the move. She had even traveled with a production show that performed in South America. The fact that she was a gypsy dancer explained her beautiful strong legs.

Without warning she turned and looked into my eyes and said, "You're a Christian, aren't you?"

I smiled.

"Can I say something to you?" she continued.

I laughed, shrugged and nodded. What she said next was beautiful.

"I challenge you to bring back to your students a love for the earth that you feel. Live with the earth on your trip. Listen to the earth. Let the water talk to you. Listen to the birds and trees and feel what they have to say. Be one with the earth."

I took the bill, and she headed towards the wash room. At her truck I held out my hand and said she would be in my prayers.

Her eyes sparkling, she exclaimed "You're not getting away with a hand shake!" She pulled me into her body. "Feel the energy of a real gypsy! Carry that energy with you on your trip!"

We smiled and got in our trucks. Jose was my first and only encounter with a gypsy.

I put down my journal and glared through the dim light of the glowing embers.

"I challenge you to listen to the earth, feel your surroundings, and record those feelings in your journals!" I pulled out thirteen journals and laid them at my feet.

The students snarfed up their new, clean, empty-paged chronicles and pounced on their first assignment. We broke up into our canoe groups and interviewed each other about our greatest fears and highest anticipations for the trip. I gave them 5 minutes for this, but we did not regroup for nearly a half hour. Four small groups were spread in the dark talking, sharing, and recording. "Maybe they would write?" I thought to myself observing how eagerly they began to scribble into their journals.

Kailee, Lindsey and I sat, talked and wrote until I could sense a gentle fatigue beginning to creep in on all of us. We gathered the group; then Chris, Diane and I established our basic safety rules. The students were off to their tents.

The boys fell fast asleep. Laughter, gross body noises and hilarity erupted from the girls' tents. One group of girls came out, took the toilet paper, and disappeared into the darkness. Screams of laughter resounded through the night. Upon their arrival back at camp, I told them I had never heard anyone have so much fun going to the bathroom. They laughed again and disappeared into their tent.

Taking Care of Business

Victoria's Journal

Go way back into the woods by myself, in the dark, alone. Right! Dig a hole with a tiny orange shovel, do my business in the hole, cover it back up and everything is cool. Right! No way! You gotta be kidding. I was scared and so were the other girls in my tent. But we had to go!!!!

We decided we would all go together. The four of us crawled out of our tent and timidly took the little orange shovel and toilet paper. Without saying a word, we passed the adults and headed out into the darkness of the night. The woods quickly engulfed us, and the security of our camp and fire was left behind. We walked up a long hill, holding hands, bunched together in a tight group. Finally we were able to get far enough away to be completely out of sight.

We found a little tree back in the woods and decided that was the spot. Our tree was about 5 or 6 feet high, had a few green leaves on it, and its bark was brown. It didn't seem real sturdy. A knotted plastic bag held our toilet paper and with our little orange shovel in hand we stood staring at the tree.

"Dig a hole," Mr. Rigby had said. "Do your business in the hole," he said. Sounds so easy, but yuck, was all I could think. We tried.

To our dismay we discovered that we were all "diggingly challenged!" We started giggling which did not help. We made the holes way too small which caused predictable results. We missed and all started laughing. Finally one girl (I won't mention that it was Kellie because I don't want to embarrass her) leaned against the tree for support. With a loud snap the tree broke. Kellie fell flat on her back in a pile of leaves. Plastered with leaves, she rolled on the ground laughing even harder. Tears of hilarity streamed down our faces.

Our business done, we covered the whole area in leaves and retreated back to camp. As we walked by the fire, Mr. Rigby asked, "What happened out there? I never heard anyone laugh so loud!"

Heads lowered so not to meet his eyes, we slammed the little orange shovel and toilet paper down at the end of the canoe table and silently dove into the security of our tent. There, we all burst into laughter. My bathroom adventures were very interesting and private from that point on!

Diane, Chris, and I finally retreated to our tents. Tina built up the fire and sipped her coffee while we all drifted off to sleep. Caves, bump bumping, white water, cliff diving, and who knows what surprises might meet us tomorrow.

8/9/04 Monday
First Breakfast

Birds calling softly and the dim light of pre-dawn woke me gently. A misty fog covered our gravel bar and totally immersed our tents in gray droplets. Chris donned his running gear while I quietly forced the air out of my cheap, dollar fifty luminescent green air mattress. Outside, Chris jogged off down a trail for his morning run. I accepted a hot cup of coffee from Tina and searched for a spot to do my Tai Chi. No words were spoken by any of us. We don't want the so disturb the peaceful silence of morning.

The sun appeared as a ghostly pale circle, veiled by the thick fog. Balanced on flat rocks at the river's edge, I focused on the sun while performing my morning ritual of circular movements and stretches. Sore muscles and stiffness from sleeping on a bed of rocks, quickly disappeared. Moving to a small ledge back behind the fire, I smiled at Diane, who emerged from her tent. She grinned a silent good morning, grabbed her fishing pole, and headed downstream. I quietly read my bible, prayed and watched the students begin to stumble sleepily out of their tents.

Tina had a large pot of water boiling on the fire. She had also opened and laid out a bag of instant hot chocolate. A bag of homemade granola that I prepare for all our trips sat open next to the chocolate on our canoe-table. Some of the students, like Bill, had smiles on their faces.

"Good morning Mr. Rigby! Sleep good?" he quipped, full of enthusiasm.

But most were grumpy. A cup of hot chocolate and a handful of granola began to change most of the frowns into smiles. Not Victoria. She sat leaning against a canoe with her long brown hair covering most of her pouting face. She is not a morning person and it would take a lot more than hot chocolate and granola to get a smile from her. We gave her space.

The first morning with this trip, as most, is an ensemble of disorganized chaos. Students need to learn camp rituals and routines that now are completely foreign to them. They don't know what to do or where anything is. The chaos is about to change. Chris has returned from his run, his body steaming in the morning chill. He had a cup of hot tang in his hand. Diane had caught no fish and was now at the fire sipping coffee. Tina was anxious to get breakfast started.

After the students had gone to bed last night, the chaperons had determined the make-up of three camp groups. Each group would have a specific task or responsibility for the day and then would switch duties the following day. In that manner everyone had an opportunity to share and contribute. Chris took the boys, who are the fire builders for today. Because we are using stoves, they also do the river study and collect BMIs (benthic macro invertebrates). Chris got them busy packing their gear and taking their tent down. After breakfast they would begin their river study.

"Where is my flashlight?" asks Ricky.

"You put it in your pack already." Answers Bill.

"Where is my tooth brush?"

"It's in your pack."

"I can't find my sun glasses!"

"They're on your head."

Ricky had a knack of losing or misplacing everything. Bill patiently helped him get organized and together they started on their tent.

Diane explained to her girls that they are K.P's. and will be doing the dishes today. They needed to get their stuff organized and packed before breakfast. Caity, Lindsey, Kailee, and Abby retreated to their tent to begin their foreboding task of cramming the mounds of clothing back into their Bill's bags. No parent help this time, they were on their own.

Tina had Kellie, Alexis, Kate and a now smiling Victoria breaking eggs and starting the breakfast. I tried to keep everything flowing smoothly and began by helping Tina. We had new stoves and cook gear. She quickly acclimated to them and got her group on task frying ham and eggs.

The sun had made its way above the tree line and was beginning to burn the mist from the river. It would be a hot day. I got the water study gear from one of our two York packs and organized microscopes, tweezers, and identification keys for Chris and his group.

This was a year in which we had purchased new equipment to replace much of our old supplies. Instead of tattered old canvas Duluth packs, we now used Bill's bags and plastic York packs. Diane and I discussed how the new cook gear would be cleaned and packed. We had coached our High School Soccer team for several years and worked together well. I knew she wanted some guidelines for handling the new equipment. I also realized she would eventually pack and do things in her own way no matter what I said. If given the opportunity, she would find the most efficient way to do things

I retreated to my tent and changed into swim trunks and sandals. Chris and I took down our tent and quickly packed our own gear. Then we set about helping the students, who were doggedly trying to get all their gear back into their small stuff sacks. Somehow amidst bantering, laughter and joking all the packs got packed.

While students were loading the canoes, I swam out to the base of a fifteen foot cliff upstream from our campsite. Treading water in the cold river I took a deep breath and dove. Strong strokes carried me to the bottom of the crystal clear water. Several deep plunges to the bottom convinced me that the area was safe and that there were no new rocks to endanger the students. Chris gathered the group together and led them into the frigid spring fed river water. Shivering from the cold water, they climbed up a rock at the base of a trail which twisted to the top of the cliff. Abby, Diane and Tina stayed down at the river with me. They had decided not to jump. I am dying to jump! My hip says no!

Chris proceeded to give a short lecture concerning cliff jumping safety. The students were glued to every word he said. Without warning he abruptly turned and jumped. The students stood alone at the top of the cliff.

Airborne (student journals)

Kate's Journal

"Oh, this is cold!" I said to myself while putting on my swim suit which was still wet from our swim last night. We walked into the calm water of the eddy pool where our canoes and kayaks were beached. The early morning mist had just cleared and the sparkling water rushed by the base of the cliffs we were about to climb. A quick swim and we pulled ourselves up on the solid rock which formed a rustic set of steps up the first part of the cliff. The path was narrow and steep as it led up and over a series of ledges. We climbed upward, occasionally using some of the weeds and branches that were trying to overgrow and cover the path, for support. When I reached the top it seemed the cliff was much higher than when I was at the bottom. My confidence evaporated and I started to get nervous.

Bill's Journal

Have you ever wanted to do something new, but were too nervous to do it? That was the way I felt while I waited my turn at the top of the cliff. Mr. Setzler explained how to jump properly so as to feel the least amount of pain. We all appreciated that, but just the fact he had to explain this made me all the more nervous. Then he asked "Bill, any facts about jumping you wish to share with us?"

I was ready.

"Any fall from over fifty feet could be fatal!"

I continued.

"Flat, calm water feels three times as hard as rough water."

In unison we all gazed over the cliff at the smooth water below. I could tell the group was very appreciative of their newly acquired knowledge by the dagger-filled glares that were cast in my direction. Mr. Setzler laughed and jumped.

He seemed to be suspended in slow motion, his body moving through the nothingness of space towards the water below. The splash that followed almost reached back up to our ledge at the top of the cliff. We were alone. No chaperones, just us. Who would be next? We all looked at each other.

Victoria stepped forward, hesitated, and after some self-reassurance, jumped. Others followed until finally it was my turn. Before I could talk myself out of it, I stepped up and jumped. The wind roared up past me, the water came at me like a speeding train. The impact, the splash, the submergence and it was over! I felt a thrill of exhilaration like I had never experienced before. This was a blast that had me craving for more. I had to do it again!

One at a time each student approached the edge, hesitated (how long depended on how much fear they were dealing with) and leapt. After his plunge, Bill came up to the surface spouting factual information.

"At fifty feet in height you would die." He informed me.

I nodded, reassured that we are safe. The cliff was not fifty feet.

Caity's Journal

Time for the main event, me, Caity; it was my turn to jump. I was scared but excited. After climbing the easy stair-like climb to the top I looked down at the water. I stepped up farther and pushed off the rock. Down I fell into the refreshingly chilly water. I loved it! I had to do it again!

Kate's Journal

I put one foot on the rocky edge and everyone behind me went silent. I was tempted to turn around, but how often do you get to jump off a cliff? I looked down at Tina to make sure she had my camera ready and pushed off. My mind screamed "Stupid Kate!"

The wind rushed at my face and than I hit the freezing cold water. I came to the surface with a smile frozen on my face. I realized the force of the landing had knocked off one of my shoes. A quick frantic search and I found it floating right next to me. I had to do it again, just like everyone except Abby and Diane. Abby had firmly stated she would not jump. While swimming towards shore with my shoe in my hand, I noticed Abby beginning her accent of the cliff, followed by Diane.

I had not noticed that Diane and Abby had left me alone. Diane had come over, whispered something quietly in Abby's ear, and they headed to shore. The two donned life jackets and had waded towards the cliff. Diane does not like heights and the year before she had refused to jump until I said, "You're probably right in not jumping. The cliff is way too high for older women and you might get hurt."

It had only taken a few minutes for her to get to the top and without hesitation she jumped!

"S—t!" she bellowed all the way until she struck the water.

She came up spouting, "I am so sorry, I did not mean to say that!"

It was ok, we were all rolling in the water laughing.

Abby was scared to death and utterly refused any of my feeble attempts to get her to jump. Somehow Diane had worked her magic and she and Abby were crossing the pool headed for the cliff.

"Yeah Ms. Dorn, you rock!" Everyone cheered when Diane jumped.

And then Abby approached. Encouragement was offered by all. She hesitated then off she flew. Bubbling to the surface she didn't say anything, but flashed a proud grin, her eyes wild with excitement. Cheers echoed off the cliff walls.

Morning Paddle

Bat Adventures

Sun tan lotion and sun block was applied while we made a final check of the camp. Sitting on the stern plate of my Grumman, I thanked our campsite with a clenched fisted salute and we were off. The cold water has cleared all heads of any sleepy cob webs. The cool crisp air was warming quickly in the sun. The different greens in the trees sparkled golden and the browns of the variegated bottom displayed pure earth colors. Our canoes sped down the river.

Our journey came to a abrupt halt around the first bend.

"Look at that giant spider web!" Yelled Kellie. "There is a great big bug in it. What the heck is that Mr. Rigby?" She questioned.

Kailee and Lindsey powered our craft around the bend and into the calm of an eddy. At first I couldn't figure it out. Then my heart almost skimped a beat at the plight of the poor hanging creature.

It was a bat. Suspended fifteen feet from an overhanging tree branch, the hapless mammal was curled up in the bright sun withering with pain. Broken fish line hung down from the branch and the treble hooks of a brilliant spinner were embedded firmly in the suspended creature's mouth. All the canoes joined together under the suffering predator to form a floating rescue platform. We had watched several bats' displaying their aerodynamic prowess at dusk last night. We could not just leave him to suffer and slowly die.

Sharp teeth, rabies, other diseases? All were factors to be considered. We needed a plan. Ricky had some thick gloves for handling fish. I had my buck knife and Kailee gave me her cup. Diane dug out needle nose pliers from her day pack.

With my canoe wedged securely in the center of our armada of boats, I stood up on the seat of the canoe, grabbed the line about a foot above the bat, and cut it. Gently I lowered the now hissing creature onto the top of my pack. I placed him in Kailee's cup and sat back to ponder my next move.

"Is that him making that noise?" inquired Kailee from her seat in the duff section. "I didn't know their teeth were so big!"

He was showing teeth, hissing, and trying to bite anything close. One of the three hooks was embedded through the upper palate or his mouth and protruded out his face. No one spoke. All fourteen of us just sat in silence feeling true compassion for this diminutive, yet feisty creature.

I could see his teeth were long enough to pierce the gloves, but felt the risk had to be taken. Using the pliers, I grasped the hook and controlled his head. With the gloved hand I gently lifted him out of the cup and onto the flat hard surface of the York pack in Chris's canoe to my left. Using the same twisting motion I would use on a hooked small mouth bass, I pushed up, twisted and pulled. The hook came free.

Liberated from the barbed hook, the bat tried flapping his wings. I released my grip and with several powerful thrusts, he was airborne. Before Chris had a chance to react the brown mammal rose into the air and whisked past his shoulder. Gaining confidence with the realization he was free, his wing beats increased in power and speed. The fortunate animal circled our floating canoes and disappeared over the tree tops. We all let out a collective gasp and just sat relishing the fact that we had just saved one of nature's most gifted pilots.

Separating, we headed down stream to explore the opening of a cave that very well could be the home that our bat was now flying towards. In little time the lead canoe floated into the deep blue pool at the end of a gravel bar. We turned right and paddled up a short tributary stream to beach our canoes in the muddy bank.

"Wow this water is freezing!" screeched Victoria.

"Clean pure spring water!" Chris and I chortled in unison.

In an effort to save wear on my artificial hip and partially metal knee, I let Chris and Diane lead the students up the rocky hillside. An easy path skirted the edge of the tumbling spring water. No one took it. Instead, they followed Chris, who scrambled straight up the rocks to the source of the spring and the closed (bat-occupied) cave mouth.

Using the "teachable" moment, Chris explained how springs and caves were formed. Realizing what he was doing, I made diagrams in the mud to reinforce his mini lecture. The students scrambled back down, took in the mud illustrations, then with a mixture of complaints and laughter waded through the cold water to their canoes. Little did they know what we had in store for them next.

Butt Bumping 101

Loaded back into the canoes, we attempted to re-enter the main river channel. Bumping boats, splashing, near capsizes and of course heaps of laughter accompanied our efforts. Lindsey remarked how she thought we might see more wild life along the river. All I could think was that no wild creature with any sense of self-preservation would be within miles of this bodacious group.

Despite our Keystone Cop like efforts, we managed to find the river and head downstream. Our next stop was Welch Spring. This spring spews out one hundred five million gallons of water per day. Efforts to use this location to build a small hospital for asthmatic patients had made a failed attempt around the turn of the 19th century.

The upstream shore, where most people stop, is loaded with stinging nettles and poison ivy. I turned our canoe to face bow first into the white-water tributary formed by the spring. Angling the bow slightly towards the opposite bank, we gently floated across the large standing waves and into the large eddy on the river left. The others followed my lead and ferried their canoes across the spring-created white water. We beached on the rocks of an island-like peninsula we have unofficially named Snake Island. It seems there is always a snake somewhere on or close to this location. I warned the students to be wary.

We hiked along the hundred yard class II rapids produced by the spring to the front of a sheer sixty foot cliff. From under its base bubbled the crystal blue waters of Welch Spring. The closed-off ruins of the failed hospital lay over-run by plants to the left. The spring is over eighty feet wide at its origin but quickly narrowed to barely twenty feet. The water than tumbles over a three foot ledge producing a white water section of currents and standing waves that merged into the main river about a hundred yards away. The unsuspecting students blindly followed Chris and I to the water's edge.

Concentrating on balancing on rocks and gathering nerve for the icy plunge, I remained silent. In the background I could hear Chris explaining the proper techniques of "butt bumping."

"Keep your feet up and your head back."

Tensed to make the leap, I heard Kate shriek "Snake!"

Snake Island rarely disappointed us. A long, brown, diamonded-backed water snake emerged from the shore grass, swam out into the clear water, and disappeared under the brilliant green water cress several feet to my left.

Concealing and attempting to control (I hate snakes!) my fear, I turned to the students and proclaim with an emotionless voice, "Water snakes aren't poisonous; they only bite the people who choose to go last!"

With that said I jumped into the rushing water and was swept away. I disappeared from the students and began an oral battle between my rational conscience and my thrill seeking spirit.

"You idiot, you were warm! Why did you jump in? Shouted my conscious.

"Cause its fun you chicken! This is great!" my spirit retorted.

"You're fifty-three you old goat! Act like it!"

"I feel thirteen, so shut up and look out for rocks!"

The power of the water hurdled my body downstream towards the awaiting rocks. Feet up and head back imitating a luge racer without a luge, I entered the rocky stretch.

"Ouch! Darn! Hope the students miss that one!" My inner self proclaimed, now working together in forced cooperation.

The water currents swept me out into the main river which we had just paddled through.

"That was great!" Exclaimed my now-unified inner self. "Now comes the real fun; the students!"

I stood up on a shallow gravel bar in the now "warm" feeling river water. Victoria emerged first. Head back as instructed, she made the mistake of leaning forward to sneak a look at her impending future. That caused her rear end to sink deeper into the water. Wham! Her body lurched upwards.

"That's why we call it butt bumping!" I shouted out to her.

Her loud laugh could be heard over the roar of the water and soon she stood by my side in the shallow water of the gravel bar.

"I have to do it again!"

She was gone, headed back up to the beginning of the spring.

Alexis emerged, then Caity and Kate; all were laughing and hanging on tightly to their fastened life jackets. Lindsey had chosen a slightly different course and she was abruptly yanked to a stop before entering the main river. She sat up with a surprised look on her face, reached under the water, and then resumed her plunging traverse towards our eddy. Laughing hysterically she stumbled towards us.

"A rock caught my shorts!" She exclaimed. "It ripped my pants!" She continued showing a two inch tear up the side seam.

"Your butt is bleeding!" howled Alexis.

"Oh no, I cut my butt!" Lindsay blurted, hardly able to talk she was laughing so hard.

Fully refreshed and re-warming in the bright sun, we loaded the canoes and paddled off to find a lunch site.

We don't carry or allow watches on the trip. I find that if given a watch, that time regulates what and when we do things. Instead, we eat lunch when we are hungry and then proclaim it to be noon. Supper is always promptly at six p.m. no matter what the real time. And, we always go to bed at nine o'clock sharp. We were hungry so it had to be noon!

Feeling my confidence growing regarding the group's canoeing ability, I let my guard down and relaxed my river vigil. This allowed Kellie and Alexis to get in front. My bad!

Wet Exit (student journals)

My Nightmare becomes reality!

We rounded a bend and the river's current drew us towards three strainers. (Strainers are my biggest fear on the river and cause many problems. They result when trees or root wads fall into the river. Water goes through the branches and sucks in anything floating. This can cause entrapment. Strainers are dangerous and should always be avoided.) The three strainers were spaced about twenty yards apart. It was too late to warn the girls so I advised Kailee and Lindsey to get ready to provide help. Kellie and Alexis were going to tip.

Kellie, who is in the stern, deftly avoided the first strainer, but was oblivious to the second until it was too late. Elfin like yelps (I would have been cursing like a wild-man) emanated from both of the hapless canoers. Their canoe crashed into the partially submerged branches. They balanced while the canoe lunged then righted itself. Strong river currents forced the canoe to dip deep into the water and the girls leaned upstream, the wrong direction. They capsized!

Kellie's Journal

We were having fun, it was our first day, and of course it had to be me and Alex! The water was flying and somehow by mistake we got in front. We tried to slow down, but no matter how hard we back paddled, the current had hold of us and we continued our flight out in front of everyone else. Like the river could not just keep going straight! It had to bend, and with the bend came the trees.

Alexis' Journal

We saw them, but just couldn't do anything to control our canoe. The current ran us straight into a log that was sticking out from shore.

"Lean towards the log Kellie!" I shouted.

I was clear out of the water and perched high up on the log. Poor Kellie leaned back away from the log. Water started flowing into our boat. We went over!

Like seasoned veterans, not the rookies they really were, they exploded into action. When Alexis burst back to surface she displayed not a bit of panic. She was mad. In a wild frenzy she tore after the floating packs. Kellie seized the canoe and when instructed, took hold of the end of the stern and let the water's power guide it safely around the third strainer. I joined her in the water and together we pulled the water-filled canoe onto the gravel bar where Kailee and Lindsey had secured our canoe.

Downstream, Alexis resembled a cowgirl chasing runaway steers. She herded the packs together and with the help of some other floaters already on the gravel bar, rounded up all the packs. Nothing was lost!

Kellie's Journal

"Get our stuff Alex!" I cried desperately while trying to hang on to the back of the canoe. We had missed the first log, hit the second, but our gear and the submerged canoe was headed straight towards a third log, the biggest of them all. The water surged under that log engulfing anything that came close. I fought desperately to keep the canoe from getting sucked under, but the current was so strong. I kept getting dragged closer and closer!

Alexis' Journal

The water tumbled me over and over like I was in a wash machine. I finally floundered to the surface.

"All our packs just fell out of the canoe. I have to catch them!" I thought and plunged into the racing water. I felt like a football player diving for a lose-ball fumble. Frantically I threw myself at the packs, jamming them towards shore and away from the logs. Looking over my shoulder I could see Kellie fighting with the canoe, losing the battle for control, but not quitting. I couldn't help her; I had to get our gear!

Kellie's Journal

"We could lose everything!" I thought while jamming my feet into the gravel bottom. The current kept dragging me and the canoe closer and closer to the approaching log.

"Help me grab the stern," I heard Mr. Rigby say. "Don't fight the current, let it help us," he continued. I couldn't believe he was actually smiling!

"Awesome, you are just toooo awesome! No panic! No quit! Cool, just cool!" he told me.

I relaxed my grip from the middle of our boat and slid to the back with Mr. Rigby. Our water filled canoe straightened with the current and we slowly let it glide towards shore and the rest of our smiling group.

"It was so scary! I was so terrified!" were my thoughts. But now everyone was laughing and we were being congratulated. I felt better, maybe even good.

Alexis' Journal

I had help! Other people were joining me in grabbing our packs from the water while I stumbled towards the gravel bar. Somehow our canoe had made it to shore, was floating, and was not water filled. My friends had Kellie's and my gear and were loading our canoe again. Mr. Rigby kept telling us we did a good job, but I didn't care. I was still mad. My towel was soaked!

Chris and Diane joined me in complementing both girls on their swift action and lack of panic. Anybody can make a mistake, we explained. It is how a person copes with and learns from a mistake that really demonstrates what kind of individual they are. These two girls were tough!

With the knowledge that our new packs all floated and kept our equipment dry, we resumed our search for a lunch site. Around the next bend was the perfect spot. A flat gravel bar with shade, deep water for swimming, and a partially submerged rock for playing; it must be noon.

1st Lunch

Lunches are always a feast for us. Tina gathered her four girls together in the shade of a big sycamore and using the upturned side of one of the York pack tops as a table; they began to gather the lunch ingredients. From the cooler came a large chunk of hard salami, a big square chunk of cheese, and turkey left from last night's supper. Chris has one lunch pack and Abby the other. Their contents include spun honey, peanut butter, drink mix, granola bars and a home made gorp (trail mix). From the bulk heads of the kayaks come the final foods which included bread, shoe string potatoes, and bananas. Tina sliced the cheese while Kelly and I worked on the hard salami. Alexis organized the bread into fourteen neat piles. Abby passed out the gorp as an appetizer. In reality it was probably about two in the afternoon. We had eaten nothing since around eight. Consequently, pieces of hard salami and cheese that are not looking "just right" disappeared into the mouths of the cooks. And Abby did more eating than passing out the appetizer. The gorp was long gone before it was sampled by the entire group.

Last night I had issued a home-run derby challenge to Chris and his canoe mates. Kailee, Lindsay and I have our "ultimate" bat which we had prepared at breakfast from a downed sycamore. Chris and Bill start a quest for their bat. Ricky took the toilet paper and little orange shovel and went off on a quest of his own.

Diane life guarded for the remaining girls who have created a multitude of games and challenges on a big rock they have discovered in the middle of the river. Their laughter completed the perfect setting for a perfect lunch site.

The Rock (student journal)

Kailee's Journal

There was a big rock in the middle of the far, deep side of the river. It was our playground while we waited for lunch. The current by shore was weak, but about half way to the rock it got real strong. Abby, Caity, Lindsey, and I struck out together, wading into the cold water.

The big rock was surrounded by a whole bunch of smaller rocks. We each climbed on a rock and stood up. The water rushed around our feet, but we could rest while standing perched over the water. The big rock was slick and the river current roared over its slightly submerged surface. I jumped from my perch towards the rock, but I was swept right over the top of it and whisked downstream. We took turns trying to conquer our rock. Each of us had the same tumble-downstream result.

I tried again. This time I jumped onto the rock and clutched my hands on a ridge sticking up from the slippery surface. Slowly I managed to get to my knees and knelt while the rushing water tried to rip me from the rock's facade. Little by little I got my feet under my body and attempted to stand. I did it! There I was standing on the rock like a surfer riding a wave; only I stayed still and the water rushed by. I started to laugh, lost my concentration and again I was tumbling downstream.

With lunch prepared, the group converged and the fourteen neat little piles of food disappeared quickly. I retreated to sit and observe the group from a short distance. I wish it were legal to lead the group in prayer. I said thanks and a little prayer to myself before laying back and drifting off to sleep for a ten minute nap.

The Fish (student journal)

Kailee's Journal

Lunch was ready, we were starved and the rock could wait! Sitting eating on the shore with our feet dangling in the water, I saw little fish everywhere. We tossed them pieces of granola, salami, and bread. They gobbled these small morsels down quickly, but couldn't be caught. I spread peanut butter on my leg to try and attract them. It worked too well

"Ouch, one bit me!" I screamed. I freaked out.

Afternoon Paddle

Stomachs full, bodies clean and refreshed, we launched our canoes back into the swift current.

"Thank you lunch site." I gave our gravel bar a fisted salute that was unnoticed by the rest of the already paddling group.

A quick paddle brought us to Akers Ferry. There are few bridges and this ferry is the only way across the river for miles. We pulled in and headed past the docked ferry boat to the little store. Six years ago we had arrived here just as a massive thunderstorm struck. The owners had allowed us to stay in the store with fifteen students for several hours, until the weather let up. Pam, one of the owners, had been a learning center director like my wife. We enjoyed chatting and now she recognizes and looks for us each year. Pam's friendly face was again there to welcome us.

Alexis and Caity found florescent pink and green baseball hats on sale for three dollars. Soon most all the girls had them. Each girl wore her hat at a different angle. They looked like they each belonged to a different ghetto-gang. (I'm not sure too many gangs wear pink florescent and green hats, however.) I almost bought one but decide pink and green were not my colors and that I would stick with my cowboy hat.

There was no bread at the store. At first I thought that was ok. We didn't need it until tomorrow and by then we would pass another store. Pam phoned to the store downstream and found they had only one loaf which they wouldn't hold for us. Now we would be short. Before I had a chance to even try and think of an alternative, another phone call was placed to a store five miles up the road. Pam informed us they would bring the bread down. That is if we did not mind waiting. Time meant nothing to us so we sat on the porch talking.

I joined the students out on the porch. They had found a cat and were giving it more attention than it had probably received the entire year. Pam came out of the store and drove off. The car at the other store would not start so she had driven off to get the bread for us.

Our whole group slowed down and let the afternoon lazily drift by. We sipped on pop, rocked on an old rocker and chatted about nothing important. Pam returned with the bread.

"No problem." She said with a smile.

Loaded down with bread, ice and the girl's new florescent hats; our lay-back crew descend back to the waiting water. We all agreed on one important item and that was that there sure were some darn good people here!

The afternoon sun was hot and we hardly went around the first bend when I rolled out of our canoe and into the cold river water. Wonderful! Kailee and Lindsay followed my lead and we floated in the water talking while clinging onto the sides of our canoe. Soon everyone was out in the water drifting. Splash fights, swimming and a bit of paddling carried us slowly along while the sun began to get closer to the horizon.

I showed Abby how to use her fist to tell how long until sunset. Holding our arms straight and making a fist with our hands, we pointed them at the sun. We concluded that it is one fist and two knuckles to sunset. That converted to about an hour and a half.

The sun can be dangerous. Sitting in a seventeen foot aluminum canoe is like sitting in a large reflector oven. Kailee, who is part Japanese, has several spots, including around her eyes, which have no pigment and required extra use of the sunscreen. These give her a mysterious look that is very complementary and exotic. (I can say that now because I am as old as her grandfather, a fact she takes the time to remind me of on a regular bases.)

Lindsey and I are pretty dark and tan easily. We competed to see who could turn the darkest. (Using #48 sunscreen we felt safe.) She is of Spanish descent. My English heritage puts me at a real disadvantage.

Lindsey looked over at Abby, who was sitting in Diane's canoe wearing two different hats, each at a different angle, and remarked

"Abby looks like a little colored girl!" she exclaimed.

I dubbed her "Lil Jemima" and Katie jumped at the chance to make up a rap. Poor quiet Abby just sat and patiently smiled while rolling her big eyes at each newly created verse. Soon Diane joins in and we were all pounding on the canoes and doing the "Lil Jemima" rap.

The opening to Cave Springs appeared on our river left.

Cave Springs

Paddling into the shade of the cliffs and with the coolness of the spring water, the temperature dropped drastically. Chris and I paddled our boats right into the cave mouth. Clear deep spring water stretched out under our canoes and the cave's darkness began to close in on us.

"Let me know where the big waterfall begins so we don't drop over it!" I whispered forward to Lindsey in the bow.

"What? A waterfall! I can't see anything! Where's my flashlight?" she howled.

Kailee started to rip into their daypack searching wildly in the total darkness while screaming at me to stop paddling. I continued moving the canoe into the blackness of the cave wall and into a large crevasse.

Wham! The sound of aluminum striking rock reverberated throughout the cave. The girls screamed while Chris and I looked at each other and smiled. Chris then told them how one year we climbed out onto one of the cave ledges and found a hole. I had taken my paddle and began to thrust it down into the blackness. I had felt no water, just something firm but soft. When we finally got a flashlight to look down the hole we found a whole family of beavers curled up, shaking in fright. I felt terrible at having poked at them.

The hole was still there, but the beavers now resided elsewhere.

2nd Camp

With the sun just starting to dip below the tree line, we pulled our canoes in on shore. Exhausted, we had stopped at the same site we used last year. Another canoe group was camped on the point across the river, but it was too late to continue and we were too tired to keep going. This would be our camp for the night.

Tina doesn't like to sleep in a tent so she started getting our "kitchen" ready. Lindsey, Kailee, and I emptied our canoe and using logs under each end to keep it stable;

established a table with a view of the river and the last rays of the sun moving up the trees on the opposite shore. All of us enjoyed the perfect "reverse" sunset while camp was set up.

Each student had their own NRS Bill's Bag pack for their equipment. These large waterproof packs had shoulder straps and handles which made them easy to get in and out of the canoes. Students had one Granite Gear compression sack for their clothes and one for their sleeping bag which left plenty of room in the Bill's Bag for other gear. We used the four-person Eureka Timberline Tents which one girl in each group was responsible to carry. The other three girls each carried food. Ricky carried the boy's dome tent and Bill had food for our breakfasts. Tired and sun burnt, everyone quietly helped each other unload and carry their packs up a steep gravel incline to our newly created camp.

All the tents were up quickly. Last night we had slept with the back of the tent a mere five feet from the river. Tonight the two girl's tents were set up on a level layer of gravel sized rock at the very tree line at the back of the site. Chris and I set up next to the boys on a point where we had sand under out tents and small rocks at the front door. Diane set up her small dome tent right next to our kitchen area in the very center of camp.

Being fire builders for the day, Chris and the boys took a canoe across the river where there seemed to be more fire wood. Tina and I got her girls ready to prepare supper while Diane and her girls brought up boats and stowed gear away. Kellie was helping me make some iced lemonade when we saw Mr. Setzler sprinting down the opposite gravel beach waving his arms like a man possessed.

***Bee Smarts** (Mr. Setzler's & student's journals)*

Chris' Journal

My boys and I were the fire builders for the evening and started out in search for firewood. There was little wood to be found around our site so acting on Mr. Rigby's suggestion, we decided to take a canoe across the river and get wood from the other side. Another group was camped downstream on the opposite shore, but plenty of wooded areas were available at a respectable distance from their campsite. Ricky, Bill and I pushed off in a canoe and drifted across.

We were in search of a "honey hole," a mystical location where dry wood could be found in a nearly infinite supply. I refer to it as mystical because I never seem to find them! This trip was no exception. Wood was scarce here also. Bill eventually wandered off alone and Ricky and I continued our search together. We discovered an upturned root wad loaded with dangling drift wood. Could it be? Could I, for the first time, have found my very own honey hole?

I approached with caution. These areas of tangled wood are also the perfect habitat for many of the assorted types of poisonous snakes found in the region. Mr. Rigby had shown me long ago how to take a piece of wood and poke and prod at the root wad to decrease the chance of a surprise reptilian encounter. I decided to make really sure that no serpentine friends would hang around so upon selection of a fine wood club, I proceeded to smack the woodpile repeatedly.

First came the sound, a loud buzzing that quickly grew into a deafening roar. Then I saw them; a black cloud emanated from the woodpile, blurring the lines that separated one branch from another. They appeared enraged! It's hard to explain how a dark cloud of swarming insects can look very angry or enraged, but somehow it was very obvious to me. Not only did I realize they were mad, but intuitively I knew they were mad at me. Real mad!

Looking back at the situation, I've been in emergency situations before and handled myself quite well thank you. I've cared for others when they had convulsions and even raced from a burning building to get help. Not this time! I screamed like a little girl, no offense to little girls, and took off running.

Ricky's Journal

I heard Mr. Setzler yell "Run!" He turned and took off with the bees chasing him. I never moved. I just stood there and watched the bees chase Mr. Setzler and I never got stung..

Victoria's Journal

"I was helping make dinner and trying not to think about how hungry I was when I heard this loud scream from the other side of the river! The whole camp stopped to turn and look at a jumping, yelling, and running Mr. Setzler. I never saw a grown man run so fast or scream so loud in my whole life!"

Chris' Journal

The cloud and sound both faded and finally there were no more insect assailants buzzing around my head. That was good. I stopped to assess the situation. I had been stung four to six times on the back of my neck and shoulders. Not being allergic to bee or wasp stings I really wasn't worried and knew the pain would pass. That was also good. Then I turned and looked across the river; our entire trip group was lined up on the shore. They had witnessed my whole embarrassing insecticidal race and were giving me a standing ovation. That was not so good.

Sheepishly I waved, bowed, and simply shouted, "Bees!"

2nd Night

Upon their return, Chris and I agreed that it was lucky that it had been him and not me. He is a conditioned long distance runner and varsity track coach. I can't run and am deathly allergic to bees.

Diane chipped in, "It would not have been me because I would not have been so stupid as to collect wood by a bee's nest in the first place!"

She can be merciless.

Alexis started browning the meat, Kellie choose to prepare the Spanish rice and Victoria, Kate and Lil Jemima prepared veggies, cheese and a salad. I finished making the ice filled juice which was devoured and replenished, devoured and replenished multiple times. When all was ready, Tina and I started browning tortillas in hot olive oil. The students lined up and served themselves tacos, rice, and salad. Nearly forty tortillas where prepared. All where wolfed down by the hungry paddlers. Darkness closed in while we sat at the river's edge eating and sharing again the events of our first day on the river.

Because of the bee attack there was no good wood for a fire. Diane had Kate, Lindsey, Kailee, and Lil Jemima busy with the hot water and dishes. I took Bill to look for wood and shortly we found another "honey hole." This spot had wood piled deep, the remnants of a previous flood and there were no bees! In the darkness we carried load after load back to camp. At the conclusion of our final trip we were greeted by a blazing fire and a cleaned-up camp.

Despite Kellie's great efforts to make perfect pudding, it still turned out runny with lumps. It didn't matter, it was consumed in seconds. Thanks to Ricky, who had reminded me at the store, we also had plenty of marshmallows. Chris sat with the bag on his lap tossing them to the hungry students who acted like seals clapping for fish. Ricky browned his carefully. Most students burnt them to a charcoal black. Lil Jemima just stuffed hers in her mouth uncooked.

The stars were magnificent! No competing lights dimmed their opulent twinkling. They spread across the night sky in regal splendor. Bill shared some more of his multitude of facts while we pointed out constellations such as Drako, the Northern Triangle and Cassiopeia. Diane had a star chart which Kellie, Victoria and she used to pick out individual stars from amongst the millions.

The fire dwindled to mere ashen coals. We were all exhausted. I was so tired I could not find a comfortable position. My legs screamed with pain. I mentioned that it may be getting close to nine and time for bed. The students disappeared into their tents and tonight there was little talk. Silence dominated the camp. The left behind chaperones made a final equipment check and left Tina maintaining her vigil next to the fire. Laying on my blown up mattress with my arms tucked under my head I watched the sliver of a moon through the back screen window. I didn't watch long and soon joined my students in a well deserved sleep.

8/10/04 Tuesday
Second Morning

I slept well, and the brightening sky outside the back of the tent woke me with peaceful ease. I leaned forward and undid the tab of my cheap air mattress and stuffed my sleeping bag into its compression sack. Then I started squeezing the squeaky mattress to remove its air. How rude could I be! I didn't even think of Chris, but soon he was up.

Tina had a rough night fighting off raccoons. Four different masked bandits tried to get our food. It was my fault. I should have made sure all the food was tucked into the York packs and that their tops were securely fastened. I had just put the food bags in a pack under the canoe. That won't happen again.

The sky was clear, and the sun was just starting to peak through the tall trees on the cliffs of the eastern riverbank. Starting my tai chi, I began to feel crabby. Then I thought-- it's a beautiful day! I'm with beautiful people!

Get it together! By the time I was done reading my Bible and praying, I felt wonderful!

Chris, Diane, and a couple of students were talking at the edge of the campsite. Diane complained that she had been disturbed by people walking by her tent in the night. I quickly stated, "Chris and I would never be so stupid as to put our tent in the middle of the camp where everybody had to walk!" Even Diane almost laughed.

Chris, Bill, and Ricky were the cooks for the day and in charge of breakfast, which I laid out on our canoe table. Homemade granola, coffee, hot chocolate, Tang, and pancake batter was spread out for preparation and consumption. Tina brought out some bananas which were still golden. I retreated to the river's edge to write in my journal and watch the camp wake up.

Victoria and Alexis are not morning people. They came out of their tents with deep scowls planted on their faces. Give them space! Kellie did not sleep well, and her face, which always is a mirror for her feelings, showed it clearly. Before anyone could say anything, Lil Jemima swooped in and gave Kellie a big good morning hug, smiled, then moved on. Bill woke up rattling off scientific facts from his infinite memory. Ricky was always looking for something he lost, as was Lindsey, who swore someone (the Mamaygwessey men) keeps taking her stuff.

Mamaygwessey Men

Kailee's Journal

Mr. Rigby told us about the Mamaygwessey Men. He said that according to Sigurd Olson, in his book The Lonely Land, the Mamaygwessey were little men with round heads, no noses, long spidery arms and legs with six fingers and six toes. Their likeness is seen on pictographs found on some cliffs in the Canadian Wilderness. These little men took gleeful pleasure in tipping canoes, disrupting camps, and misplacing items. They would steal your things for a while and then give them back, but in a new location. Lindsey and I got more than our fair share of dealing with them.

Our first encounter was when Lindsey couldn't find her camera. Her camera was missing for the entire afternoon. She was freaking out and yelling at me, "Kailee, where is my camera! Give it back!"

I had no idea where it was, but all I could do was laugh because she was really funny to watch when she freaked out. She would yell, pound her fists, and blame me. I told her, "Are you sure you looked through your whole entire bag?"

Rolling her eyes in exasperation, Lindsey disgustedly replied, "Of course!"

I was sitting in the middle of the canoe, and it was not like I had to paddle anyways, so I took her bag and started looking for her camera. I dumped the bag out by taking every crammed piece out one by one. At the bottom, I came across a camera that looked just like Lindsey's. Well, like it was hers!

Before Lindsey could yell, say thanks, or reply at all,

Mr. Rigby told us about the Mamaygwessey. We had many encounters with them throughout the entire trip, especially Lindsey and Ricky. (I still like to blame the Mamaygwessey even now that I'm back home. They are very convenient; I just wish my teachers would buy my story!)

The students continued to wake and come out of their tents. Kate is quiet but always finds ways that she can somehow help. Caity always has a big smile matched only by Kailee who is bound to trip, fall, or knock something over and then burst out laughing. Our crew was up.

While the girls sipped on hot chocolate and nibbled granola, Chris and the boys started the pancakes. The first batch is burnt, runny, and edible only by Diane. I slid in next to Bill, turned the heat down, and took the smoking pan off our Coleman stove. Quoting a Canadian guide I once worked with on the shores of Lake Superior, I explained, "Coleman stoves have two settings--off and blast off." I continued, "Take the pan off the flame to cool, add some more flour to your mix, and make each pancake a bit smaller."

Having guided for years, I quickly turned out four golden brown cakes which stimulated the girls to begin to scramble for plates. Retreating again to my journal, I watched Bill and Ricky produce golden cake after pancake with only an occasional burn.

After breakfast, Diane took her girls to a part of the river just above our camp that was running shallow and fast. This riffle area of the river was the perfect location to do our river and B.M.I. study.

Yesterday, while collecting B.M.I.'s at our campsite, Chris and the boys had little luck on their first attempt. They had recruited the girls to help. Wading back into the river, Chris laid a layer of rocks on the bottom of the kick seine net which was held by Ricky and Bill. Four girls stood dancing our "river dance" in a tight square above the net. Hips gyrating, they dug their feet into the rocks and shook loose anything clinging to the cobble sized pebbles. Victoria and I scooped up larger rocks and rubbed their surface clean with our hands.

Rushing water plowed through the net, and soon crayfish were in abundance trying to climb over the top of the net. Small fish were plastered against the mesh. Our excitement grew when we lifted the net out of the water and found hundreds of squirming little critters referred to as BMIs (benthic macro invertebrates).

On shore everyone made a mad scramble to grab tweezers and help transfer the diminutive creatures to our identification tray. Cries of "cool," "awesome," and "yuck" spontaneously blurted from everyone. The microscope was used to verify that the alleged stone fly really had two claws at the end of each foot, therefore confirming its identity. Dobsonfly nymphs (hellgrammites) with their wicked pinchers, wriggled in our collection tray next to mayflies, aquatic worms, and scuds. Right-handed snails were separated from left-handed snails while Chris and Bill recorded everything. Our final tabulation, using the Friends of the Fox River rating system, was a twenty—meaning very good, just one step from excellent. These results would be used by Chris and me next spring in our classrooms.

Diane, who has been a long-time river watch participant, today had her team of Alexis, Kellie, Kate, and Victoria organized and precise in their collection. Again, all camp activity ceased, and everyone curiously joined in to witness the results. Although some of the critters were different, a very good rating of twenty was established and recorded.

Alexis and Kellie still looked grumpy.

"Follow me girls! We gotta wake you two up and get a smile back on your faces!"

They followed me into the rushing water to do the "Super Man" log grab. The location was perfect. Water rushed over a partially-buried log creating a trough of deep, fast water behind it. I demonstrated. Grabbing the log with one hand and clinching the other fist, I flopped into the water. Doing my best Christopher Reeves imitation, I allowed the water to scream past me, creating the illusion I was flying superman fashion. Alexis, then Kellie, followed my lead into the icy cold water. Each burst to the surface with frowns replaced by ear-to-ear grins and laughter.

It was time to hit the river! We gathered at our loaded boats, and I read the following from my journal:

Lindsey's Fears (recorded Sunday night) – *Lindsey answered right away about camping and fear, "I'm ok with camping; everything is new so I'm not worried. Caves -- caves are what scare me. I'm scared of getting stuck in small places. I feel I get hyper and almost claustrophobic."*

Her eyes glanced downward when she said this, almost as if she could feel the closeness of the cave coming in and closing around her.

I asked her about fear of the river or canoeing. Eyes straight ahead she said, "I'm confident in canoeing; I feel really good about it. It's fun."

Cliffs? Her eyes focused upward as if she were trying to picture herself standing on the edge of a cliff, looking over at the rushing water. "I'm a bit anxious, but not scared or afraid, but that might change when I get there."

Kailee's Anticipation – *Kailee's giant eyes sparkled with excitement when asked this question. She had her answer ready right away and without hesitation she exclaimed, "Cliffs, jumping from high places, that is what I'm looking forward to. I love the adrenaline rush and can't wait!"*

"Today we do caves." I continued. "Make sure you have your flashlights ready to use."

Then I read this quote, "Some people regard discipline as a chore. For me, it's a kind of order that sets me free to fly." Julie Andrews, singer — Sound of Music.

Morning Paddle

With my clenched-fist salute thanking our campsite completed, we paddled off. Lindsey and Kailee were now in our Carolina kayaks being guided by Tina. Victoria and Kate were my two new canoe mates. Victoria is awake and past her morning grouchiness. Her persistent laughter and large smile make her a real pleasure to paddle with. Kate is very strong and has lots of stories to tell. We paddled close to the people who had been camping across the river from us.

"Hope we weren't too loud for you last night," I called out to the family who were just beginning to load their canoes.

"Not at all; we didn't even realize you were there," they replied.

Obviously they had missed Chris's race with the bees, and it turned out they were from our state and lived not too far from our hometown. They appreciated our gesture, a factor that would prove useful later in the day.

"My pack seems to be getting smaller every day," moaned Rickie as Chris pulled his canoe even with ours. "That, or I am getting more stuff. I just can't get everything into the bag!"

In the front of their canoe, Bill just shook his head and rolled his eyes. He had patiently helped Rickie pack and get organized again this morning.

"Look at that big rock!" pointed out Victoria. "Could we?"

Hardly a half hour of paddling had gone by. The river bent and slowed into a deep aqua blue pool that swirled gently around a monstrous rock. We could not resist, and soon canoes were beached and we were swimming out across the pool towards the rock.

The water at the base of the rock was over twenty feet deep. The rock protruded upward at nearly a sixty-degree angle. It offered few foot or hand holds. I tried climbing it but peeled off and landed flat on my back in the now, very refreshing water. Determined, I tried a different approach and carefully pulled myself up on a small ledge at the base of the large rock.

"Grab my hand!" I said.

My wet feet had made the rock surface slippery, but first Victoria, then Kate gasped my hand and pulled themselves up and onto the ledge. They followed me right up the slanted surface to the top, nearly twenty feet from the water. The side and back of the boulder dropped straight off into the shallow, boulder-strewn water. We perched precariously, facing down the steep incline looking into the deep, swirling river.

"I wanta jump! I wanta jump!" pleaded Victoria.

"No way!" I answered. "We're gonna dive!"

Tina had remained behind to take pictures from the gravel bar on the opposite side of the pool where we had parked our canoes. Ricky and Diane moved along the shore casting for small mouth at the end of the pool. Diane soon had one but Ricky remained fishless.

By now everyone else had joined us at the top of the monstrous boulder. Chris had brought a rope to make the climb easier, and even Abby (Lil Jemima) was anxiously waiting to dive.

"Watch how I do this, and make sure you jump clear of the rock," I instructed.

About half way down the rock was a small shelf that made a great diving platform, and the water was so deep that I have never even been able to swim deep enough to see the bottom. Standing on the small ledge, I launched myself with the elegance (in my mind only) of an Olympic diver and flew from the rock, plunging deep into the water. Alexis stood next on the ledge, smiling down at me trying to stifle a laugh at my pitiful effort.

"Nice dive, Mr. Rigby!" she is always so polite, but a poor liar.

Alexis is long and athletic, and with true grace she dove hardly making a splash when she entered the water. Soon everyone was throwing their bodies into the deep cool waters of our pool. Only Lindsey had trouble.

"I can't do this!" she said while scrambling back to the top.

"I have to do this!" she scrambled back down to the ledge.

"I can't, I can't!"

The first night she had stated that she did not have a fear of diving from the cliff, but that might change when she actually got there. Now she was arguing with herself, trying to gather the courage to leap.

"I can! I can't! I can! I can't!"

"Noooooo!"

She seemed to almost run down the side of the rock and belly womped into the water.

Each of us dove a last time and swam back across the deep water to the gravel bar and our waiting canoes. Lindsey and Kailee had not enjoyed being in the kayaks and wanted to rejoin me in the canoe. Caity and Victoria took the kayaks, and I welcomed my canoe mates back to our boat.

The next stretch of river had several strainer-strewn shoots to negotiate. Lindsey and Kailee pointed out rocks and together we navigated safely. At the end of each shoot we steered our boat into an eddy and helped direct the rest of the canoes and kayaks. First Tina and the kayakers, then Diane, followed by Kellie and finally Chris; each watched carefully then negotiated safely. Not really dangerous, just fun. We beached our canoes without mishap at the Pulltite campground landing to replenish our water and pick up fresh ice for our drinks that night.

A misplaced clock on the wall behind the counter of the small store said it was 12:15. Without hesitation, I told the students Pulltite was using Ozark Mountain Time, which is two hours different than ours and that it was really just 10:15. Kailee nodded in agreement. We headed back to the river to complete our "morning" paddle.

This was an exploring day. We pulled in again after only a short distance to hike up to Pulltite Spring itself. It was just a quick hike to the base of the cliff where 47 million gallons of water emerged each day. We stood peering deep into the crystal clear pool where we could actually see the bubbling water percolating up from the depths below.

We took a diversion on the way back to the river, and using a seldom traveled, difficult to locate trail, hiked to the top of the bluff above our canoes. Having already explained how the Ozark Mountains had formed due to a gigantic batholith, I offered a prize.

"Whoever is first to find evidence proving that this bluff was once the bottom of an ocean gets a milkshake!"

Students spread out in a wild quest. Through red pines and over large boulders, the students searched in the hot sun.

"Here they are! Here they are! This used to be a beach!" howled Kate.

Standing directly on the ripple marks in the dolomitized limestone, Kate proclaimed the milkshake as hers. She was justified, her second shake of the trip. The ripple marks were a clear geologic indicator that this mountain top had once been the shore of a huge body of water.

Next, I explained about lichens (fungus-like plants) and described the brilliant red features of a species commonly referred to as British Soldiers.

"Whoever finds a British Soldier gets another milkshake!" I challenged again.

"Here's one!" announced Ricky.

"No, that's orange, not red," I pointed out.

"This is it!" he announced again.

"No, but close."

"How about this?"

"Is this it?"

Ricky made a Herculean effort identifying every substance with even the slightest hint of red as the sought after lichen. Still we found none. This year we came up empty and descended to the river without being able to find the brilliant red lichen.

Splashing our way back to our canoes, we didn't bother to even get in, but just floated next to them while crossing to the gravel bar on the other side. Removing life jackets, donning shirts, and retrieving flashlights from our water bags, we headed into the woods to explore the challenges of the Sink Hole Cavern we had dubbed Mudder Cave.

Mudder Cave (student journals)

Victoria's Journal

As we approached the cave, I could feel the temperature drop. I started to shiver from the coldness and because I had little butterflies in my stomach. At the mouth we stood listening to Mr. Setzler give us a safety talk. We were all nervous, especially Lindsey and Kellie. I didn't understand why Mr. Rigby called it the mudder cave. When asked, he just smiled and said, "Nice white shirt Victoria," and left to wait for us at the other end.

My legs don't let me do caves anymore, but this is where Chris and Diane really excel. Leaving Tina, her feet blistered from cheap aqua socks, to watch the canoes, we headed up a trail, back into the woods. Slowly, we worked our way up the sig-saging switch backs towards the top of one of the "Ozark Mountains." Near the very top, we broke off from the trail and headed down a steep ravine that led to the mouth of the cave.

The cave entrance resembled the gaping mouth of a giant whale with a small stream seeping through its jaws. Late summer drought had reduced the stream to only a small trickle of water. The large opening quickly narrowed and disappears into the darkness. Chris explained that this passage will converge to a very "tight" tunnel. The only way to make it through is to turn your head to the side, outstretch your hands above your head, and push with the tops of your feet.

Apprehension and fear was so thick I felt I could almost cut it with a knife. Kellie and Lindsey were especially nervous. Diane, who is a very "shapely" young woman, relieved the tension when she stated. "I just push really hard and everything flattens out!"

Giggling nervously, the group disappeared into the darkness.

Abby's Journal

"What's that noise?" I uttered to no one just after we started into the blackness of the cave. Turning my flashlight to the ceiling, I discovered finger-sized crickets. Hundreds of them occupied the cracks and ridges of the jagged ceiling. I moved on, ducking my head a bit lower.

Sitting in the quiet, alone on the hill at the sink hole exit, I could not help but marvel at the wonderful job of guiding the students that Chris and Diane did. As stated earlier, Chris had been a student of mine in the eighties, and we have worked together for ten years teaching science. I had first met Diane years ago when she had the reputation of being the meanest, yellow-card-issuing referee of our soccer league. I had made it my unsuccessful quest to make her smile. We had become close friends after working together at an outdoor education class where I discovered her true personality included a brilliant mind and a great sense of humor. She actually could and did smile often! Presently, she is a high school science teacher at a nearby school. Now the two of them were guiding the petrified students through the total darkness and the very tight passages of the Mudder Cave.

Kate's Journal

We could walk upright at first, but that soon changed. We stooped and then got on our knees and began to crawl. The cave got smaller, forcing us onto our stomachs. We had to wait in the total dark for the people in front to get through the first tight spot. The rocks scraped at my back and stomach, and we were forced to turn our heads sideways to fit. Kellie got her butt stuck and began to cry.

"Just relax. If I can make it, so can you," reassured Ms. Dorn.

Some of the students had head lamps; most had flash lights that they carried when convenient. But, they had to jam them in their mouths when the cave got tighter and they were forced to crawl. Chris led the way while Diane brought up the rear. The students worked together, offering encouragement to each other as the cave ceiling narrowed and the bottom became covered with cold mud and clay.

Kailee's Journal

Victoria asked, "Hey, Kailee, if I put my hands where your feet are and supported them, would that help you?" I already had my hands behind Kate's feet giving her support. "It sure would! Thanks," I replied. Kate had her hands behind the feet of Alexis. The person behind would put their hands out so you could push off them with your feet. Otherwise, your feet just slid in the mud. In this manner we helped each other to inch-worm our way through the really tight sections.

"Wow it's bigger this time!" announced Mr. Setzler.

"Big? How could this be big? He's crazy!" I thought to myself.

The students had moved several hundred yards back into the mountain and were slowly crawling upwards towards the sinkhole where I was waiting. The sinkhole had formed when the cave itself, which was actually an underground stream, had neared the surface enough so that the top collapsed. It formed a large round hole that led straight down to the cave.

Everyone has different fears, and each person faces those fears in their own way. Lindsey had stated that she feared caves, and now she and the group were facing those fears together.

Abby's Journal

"It's okay, Lindsey; we're almost to a cavern where you can sit up," I said in attempt to comfort her. Although quietly crying, Lindsey had a determined look. With Mr. Setzler's added reassurance, she wiggled forward. Sitting up in the small relieve of a diminutive cavern, we could see a slight smile slip onto Lindsey's mud-streaked face."

Kate's Journal

Mr. Setzler wiggled through the next hole followed by Ricky and Bill. I was next and got through easily until my shirt got caught. I wiggled and pushed, but was stuck.

"You're never gonna get through!" teased a laughing Alexis.

"Oh yeah! Let's see how you do!" I taunted back, now free and sitting up.

Kailee's Journal

I braced her feet and Alexis slipped right through. Then it was my turn. It was more muddy than rocky, and I couldn't go anywhere because my feet kept slipping. I began to panic. It felt like I was having a baby or that I was the baby trying to get out! I pushed and pushed, and foot by foot I slowly forced my way through the torturous passage guided by Mr. Setzler's confident voice. He relaxed me just as he did each of us.

"Ok now, watch your head, Kailee. Don't stand up," he informed me, and then I was through.

"Now, Victoria, be careful of your head; turn it to the side," he continued with his consoling advice.

At the sinkhole, Kate's head emerged first. She climbed out to join me where I sat at the rim of the gaping hole. Alexis and Victoria, who were plastered with mud, came next.

"That was so awesome!" both exclaimed with white teeth flashing in contrast to their mud-streaked faces. They were pumped with excitement and thrilled at what they had just accomplished.

"Did you know that all caves have a temperature of ..." Bill's head popped up, and he told us some fact about cave temperature. Then he disappeared, determined to follow the cave tunnel in the opposite direction.

Climbing out of the sink hole was no easy task, and Kellie was having trouble.

"There are directions how to climb out of the cave written in the rock right next to your right elbow," I chided.

Kellie lowered her arm and looked. "Mr. Rigby!" she rolled her eyes in disgust.

Abby's Journal

We could stand and we could even see light from above. But, the adventure wasn't over just yet; we still had to get out of the sinkhole. Lindsey went first. She couldn't find a foot or hand hold and started to get scared that we wouldn't be able to get out at all. There was a small hole at the top of the rim opening. Leaves started to fall from it right into Lindsey's face. She got mad, grabbed the rocks, and pulled herself up and out of the cave.

I still don't know how I managed to get out, but when I did, I found Lindsey sitting on a rock with the biggest smile I had ever seen. I could hear Kellie laughing and then I looked at everyone. We were all covered from head to toe with mud. Victoria was the dirtiest, her new white shirt filthy.

All had made it! Never before on any past trip had every single student been able to work their way through the "mudder" cave. With ten cameras lined up to my side,

I had the twelve muddy spelunkers group together for pictures.

Victoria's Journal

"Nice white shirt, Victoria," stated a smiling Mr. Rigby.

Looking down at myself, I clearly understood why it was called the Mudder Cave.

Returning to the canoes, I was fully aware that Chris and Diane had done a lot of coaxing and confidence building to get everyone through. New bonds were being built and strengthened between students and teachers. These were relationships that would be remembered and cherished long into the future and after our trip.

Upon arrival at the river, everyone jumped in to clean off and cool down. Remembering that the clock at the campground store had read twelve fifteen; I knew in reality it was probably late afternoon.

"Wow, lunch is late," I proclaimed. "It must be 12:05. Mr. Setzler, do you think you and the boys could possibly find us a lunch site?"

Chris, who is a food-consuming factory, had the lunch ingredients in his canoe. No reply was necessary, and his canoe soon ripped off through the water. He and the boys quickly disappeared paddling wildly down river.

2nd Lunch

We found them at a site where I had once camped in 1977. The York pack was out, opened, and lunch was almost ready.

On the river left, the water danced and sparkled over a series of boulders. Diane quickly had most of the girls' feet up, head back, butt bumping through the white water. I couldn't help but join them, and we all played together in the cold water. Caity slipped and fell, showing everyone how to "body" bump. She bounced and rolled over the rocks finally emerging in the deep pool at the end of the shoot, laughing.

Body Bumping (Butt Bumping Extreme!)

Caity's Journal

"Wait for me, Kailee!" I shouted across the racing whitewater. Racing whitewater for sure, this was the fastest water I had ever seen.

We had stopped for lunch and a little break. Mr. Setzler and the boys were making lunch. We slammed down some gorp and then headed out into the rapids led by Ms. Dorn. After yelling for Kailee to wait, I hopped into the water. It was really hard to keep my balance and not fall. I tip-toed cautiously. I could see Kailee and Lindsey were already launching their bodies into the water and being hurled downstream. What were they thinking? Sharp rocks were everywhere!

"Ow!"

The jagged rocks kept banging at my legs. I tried desperately to catch up. Wham I was down! The water had tackled me, and I was now firmly in its grasp.

"Ouch! My butt!"

A large rock pounded me. All control was gone; the river hurled me into rock after rock, each causing new pain at different spots on my legs. Frantically, I flailed my arms in a mad attempt to get a grip on something, anything to stop my tumbling ascent through the painful rocks. It was useless. I couldn't fight the current, so I tried dodging the rocks, hoping the river would lead me to a softer, less painful spot.

It did. I was in the deep safe water at the end of the rocky run. But now everyone was moving back up the riverside to the beginning of the very run I had just thrashed my way down! Floundering out of the water, I raced to catch up. At the head of the run, I caught Alexis and grabbed her arm. Tripping, I was again back in the powerful swirling water. Still clutching Alexis's arm, I pulled her down with me.

"Yes! This is better!" were my gleeful thoughts.

I started my plummeting aquatic ascent again, but this time I was not alone.

Leaving Diane and the girls in the white water, I joined Lil Jemima, who had found her own deep powerful pool behind a submerged log. Lindsay and Kailee had taken residence in a shady spot and were feverishly working on their journals. They were joined by others, and soon five students were quietly immersed in writing. They sat absorbing the sights, sounds, and smells around them while trying to extract their feelings onto their paper. The boys called that lunch was ready.

This group, despite being mostly girls whom I found usually eat less, could really put the food away. They had consumed nearly forty tacos the night before, and now we discovered that almost our entire supply of spun honey had been devoured at the first lunch. They were already into the second jar of peanut butter, and gorp seemed to vanish into the air. Everything edible soon disappeared. The last pieces of crumbled cheese, left over salami, and bread heels were quickly "horse-n-goggled" off.

(Horse-N-Goggle)

Mr. Rigby's Journal

"Eine, zwei, drie, horse-n-goggle," I stated to begin the raffle. Students then flash as many fingers as they wish from zero to five, but not more than five, because they don't have more than five. The total number of fingers is quickly tabulated. Counting clockwise around the group, each student is counted until the student that matches the tabulated total is reached. That student is the winner. We have settled arguments, debates, and who gets the "left-overs" in this manner for years.

Bill and I napped in the shade, but only after he informed me about some fact concerning the sun and solar flares. Again I told him, "Bill, I wish I had a tape recorder to record all your facts. I could write an encyclopedia and be rich!"

Many girls wrote in their journals; then all of us shampooed and cleaned up. Shadows were getting long and the sun was nearing the tops of the trees. I decided we had better finish "lunch" and move on. We still had another cave to explore.

While loading the canoes, Diane yelled, "Kailee, stop!"

Kailee froze. She had almost walked into the same shiny lure we had extracted from the bat's mouth yesterday. Ricky now had it tied at the end of his fishing pole.

"Wow! Thanks, I almost walked right into that," Kailee stated.

She promptly turned, picked up her life jacket and before we could shout a second warning, walked right back into the same lure.

While Bill was stating some fact concerning the memory length of fish, Diane used the pliers to remove the hook, which had only caught cloth, not flesh.

Afternoon Paddle

Kellie and Alexis were getting tired paddling by themselves, so Chris started training Bill to do the stern. Alexis and Caity took the kayaks. Kate helped Kellie paddle with the promise they would both get a rest as soon as Bill was proficient enough.

We usually spend over an hour in the next cave. We have named it the "Challenge" cave. It was still an hour or more away. It was then another hour to our usual campsite at Sinking Creek. The sun was getting very low.

Alexis proved to be a very strong kayaker and an even better splasher. Poor Caity could neither match Alexis in speed, nor did she know how to splash. Alexis would pound her with water then paddle quickly away. Caity, with her florescent pink and green hat cocked to the side, would give chase. Alexis let her get close and then resumed her onslaught of water across and over Caity. Caity would stop and give a pitiful effort at a splash whereby Alexis would paddle off completely dry. The whole group rocked with laughter as Alexis continued her thrashing of Caity.

Finally Caity grabbed the bilge pump and exclaimed, "Now you've had it!"

A weak six-inch-long trickle of water emerged pitifully from the end of the pump. Laughing so hard I almost fell from my perch on the stern plate of my canoe, we watched as Alexis resumed her merciless pounding of the drenched but persistent Caity.

Less than half an hour to the cave, Bill took over for Kellie. She finally got a well-deserved rest. Chris and I decided we would try and camp on the small gravel bar across from the "Challenge." The sun was very low. In the shadows of dusk, we rounded the rapid-strewn bend and using the strong eddy, pulled into the gravel bar. Someone was already camped there.

3rd Camp

We pulled in anyway; we had no choice. The students sat in their canoes while Chris, Diane, and I gathered to discuss options. We had three choices. One was to skip the cave and go on to find a different campsite. Two, we could do the cave and find a campsite in the dark. Three, we could explain our plight to the other campers, set up camp, and do the cave after dark. Unanimously, we choose number three.

I walked over to where the campers were seated comfortably watching the sunset. To my surprise, I found them to be the same people we had camped across from last night. How fortunate that we had apologized to them earlier this morning. They were very understanding and had no problem with us sharing their small gravel bar. They didn't want the students to miss the cave.

"The only fun thing our science teacher ever did was to burn some marshmallows!" exclaimed their eighth grade daughter. Chris and I smiled.

Relieved, I walked back and explained the situation to the students. We were all excited about exploring the cave at night, and tents were going up in minutes. Chris and I lined up our timberline with the two girls' tents using the side fly ropes to lash the tents together. Our tent doors were a mere five feet from the gurgling water. Our tent rears butted up to the trees at the edge of the small gravel bar. Canoes were placed at both sides of the tents to support the outer sides. We had a very tight secure camp.

Diane and the boys each had pop-up domes that they set up on a flat, sandy ledge back from the river. A large downed tree at the river's edge made a perfect table for our kitchen. The York packs were placed at its base. In the growing darkness, we set out to find fire wood.

Diane and Tina led most of the students up a trail back into the woods. I went solo upstream along the river hoping to find another "honey hole" of left-over flood debris. Climbing a very steep sand bank, I found just such a spot.

There was more than enough wood for the entire night and morning, but I could not carry it down the steep bank and back to camp. Returning for help, I found Diane and the girls all sitting in the water. Before I could ask what was going on, Diane turned, and with a sour, hurt look said, "Nettles!"

Nettles (Urtica Dioica, Itch Weed, The Plant of Pain!)

Caity's Journal

"Wow!" I thought. "We are camped right outside a cave, separated only from its entrance by the fast moving current of the river itself. Tonight we would explore it! How cool could this be?!"

It was starting to get dark already, and we needed fire wood. I followed Kailee, Lindsey, and Abby while Ms. Dorn led us back into the woods. We scrambled up a narrow trail through dense trees and brush right behind our tents. We immediately encountered a steep sandy hill. On all fours, we scrambled to the top where we spread out in search of wood.

It was dark, warm, and gloomy; there were so many plants and trees. I kept my eyes wide open and alert, not only for fire wood, but for poison ivy. We split apart, yet stayed close enough so that no one would get lost.

"Yes!" I thought to myself. "Here is a good chunk of wood!"

I walked a bit further, alert, watching for any ivy. I walked into a dark green bush and thought nothing of it because it wasn't ivy. I was okay, like, so I thought…

Abby's Journal

Ms. Dorn said, "Abby, you stay here and look for wood."

The others moved off, and I stayed at the top of the hill. I was gathering some little sticks when I walked into some dark green plants. A sharp pain shot up my leg. Stopping, I nervously looked down fully expecting to see blood, a spider, or even a snake. Nothing! Seconds later, my leg started to itch so bad it felt like there were a hundred mosquito bites all in the same place. I tried to itch it, but my whole ankle was burning, and I had no idea how to make it stop!

Caity's Journal

"Ouch! It itches and stings!" I yelled at Ms. Dorn, as she, Kailee, and Lindsey came tearing out of the woods.

Without stopping for an explanation, Diane yelled, "Don't itch it, Caity! Just follow me!"

I stopped itching and joined the others in a race to the water. We passed a scratching Abby, who also stopped her itching, and tore off with us towards the river.

Ms. Dorn hit the water without breaking stride. All four of us were hot on her heels. Finding a large submerged rock, she sat with most of her body immersed. The burning was almost unbearable, but we each found our own rock and sat in the frigid water.

Abby's Journal

"Don't itch it; it will make it worse. Just sit down and soak your legs until the stinging stops and DON'T SCRATCH!" instructed a calm, but thoroughly peeved Ms. Dorn.

While sitting miserably in the water, Ms. Dorn explained, "Nettles are a green leafy plant with little stingers that look like fish hooks. Some people eat the leaves like lettuce or even make tea from them."

Mr. Rigby came back to the campsite and yelled, 'What's going on?"

Ms. Dorn simply replied, "Nettles."

Mr. Rigby nodded, smiled, and then began to laugh. We didn't think anything was funny. I'll never touch stinging nettles again!

I needed no further explanation. I knew from experience that the stinging burn from nettles is awful. But they all looked so pitiful I could not help but start laughing. Soon I was joined by everyone but the doleful girls in the water.

Lesson learned, everyone followed me to the honey hole. We formed a long line and relayed the wood back. I pulled wood from the gnarled pile and handed it to Diane. She tossed it over the bank down to Bill. He then loaded others who followed a path back to camp where they gave it to Chris and Tina. Tina would have been satisfied to just make one large jumbled pile. Not Chris. He made sure Tina broke each piece to the same approximate length and then piled them in separate piles depending on their size. He is so anal! (I do the same thing, but that's ok.)

With darkness upon us, we devised an exciting plan. We would ferry the students across the river to the cave. It wouldn't matter what time it was because it was dark in the cave anyway. No one was terribly hungry because we had just eaten lunch. Plus, according to our time we had not eaten supper so it wasn't even 6:00 P.M. (Right! It was probably pushing 9:00!)

Flashlights were gathered and life jackets put on. Tina and I would prepare supper while Chris and Diane led the students through the cave. Four students jumped in my canoe, and using the strong current, I ferried across the river to the entrance of the cave. Dropping those four off, I came back and got four more. Upon return, Chris took one student and Diane another. Watching what I had done, they expertly ferried them across. Soon their waving flashlights and babbling noise disappeared into the hillside. Silence, except for the ever present mumbling of the water.

Tina and I had time to organize all the food and equipment before starting the meal. Sitting with our backs to the log, facing our stoves and the open water, we began supper. Tina prepared the boiling water for macaroni and cheese. She also set about putting together a humongous salad. I made fruit drink and started working on the forty hot dogs.

With the meal almost ready, Tina disappeared to clean up and relax. Just as I finished draining the noodles and covering the last cooked hot dog, the students began to emerge from the cave.

Challenge Cave (student journals)

Bill's Journal

Tents were up. The sun was almost down. We were exhausted. But our lust for a challenge and our desire to compete had not been quenched. Directly across the river from the front door of our tents gaped the sinister opening of the cave. Somewhere back in the bowels of the earth we would be asked to do horizontal climbing over an icy, cold spring. That was the challenge we had heard about all week long. The vote was unanimous. We loaded into the canoes and were ferried across the river.

Kailee's Journal

We assembled in the mouth of the cave. Mr. Setzler again gave us a safety talk. Don't fall into holes; don't hit your head, blah, blah, etc, etc. Heard it before.

The rock strewn entrance to the "Challenge" cave is found at the bottom of a sheer seventy-foot cliff on the outside portion of the river. The river rips through the jagged rocks and only small eddies can be found to land the canoes. A rough thirty foot climb brings the students to the mouth of the cave. Like the Mudder Cave, this cave is formed by underground, flowing water and it starts muddy and very slippery. The ceiling for the first several hundred yards is nearly forty feet high. With flashlights in hand or on heads, the group started its exploration.

Victoria's Journal

I thought it would be just a giant opening that contained a big cavern. I was wrong. We started walking in ankle deep water, the top of the cave towered above our heads. The water depth increased slowly, and the cave ceiling descended.

"What's that noise?" We all thought the same thing.

The crashing sound of rushing water could be heard in the near distance.

"A waterfall in a cave?" we questioned.

And there it was, a seven foot wall of water shooting over a ridge in the cave wall. Up we went, climbing next to the powerful cascading water. The cave leveled off, and we continued our journey.

After the waterfall, the cave narrows to about ten feet in height. Its ceiling glistened with thousands of pencil sized stalactites. Stalagmites rise from the floor and on the walls. Where the two meet, they form columns some of which are so large that the students have to squeeze through just to keep going. The floor of the cave is covered with a foot to three feet of water that is treacherous to walk through. Unseen ridges followed by deep holes trip and tear at the students' legs.

Kailee's Journal

I kept hitting my head on stalactites that were clinging from the cave ceiling, forgetting to lower my head down far enough.

(I'm not as short as I used to be.) The first bang on my head hurt a lot. Soon I felt like a pin ball in a pin ball machine; my head ricocheted off rocks at least twenty different times. After awhile I got used to it.

The dreaded drip holes were a different story. The constant dripping of water caused water-filled holes to form that were as deep as two feet. Diane had told me about a billion times to make sure I picked up my feet or I would trip and fall. She should have told me a billion and one. Hooking my foot on the edge of a drip hole I tumbled head first into the cold cave water. Mr. Setzler's blah, blah safety lecture made a whole lot of sense now. I was freezing from head to toe and covered with goose bumps.

At times the cave ceiling gets so low the students are forced to bend with their faces almost in the water. Other times they are forced to climb up onto ledges along the cave wall. After what seems to be about a quarter of a mile, the cave narrows, and the students nervously climb up above the water and along the cave walls. The water appears to disappear, but it can be seen through small gaping holes. Eventually, the passage narrows to one small hole just big enough for a body to slide through. The challenge lies on the other side.

Bill's Journal

Wading through the water, ducking stalactites, and climbing through drip holes with our flash lights firmly grasped between clenched teeth, we reached a point where the water disappeared under a solid wall of cave formations. We were forced to climb up onto a shelf ridge.

"Put your back against the one wall and your feet on the other," Mr. Setzler instructed us.

Twelve goose-bumped-covered bodies shimmied between the cave walls to a small opening. Head first, each of us wedged through the hole and slid the ten feet back to the floor of the cave. We had arrived. This was the cavern where the "Challenge" would take place.

"Turn off your lights!" demanded Mr. Setzler.

My mind screamed in disbelief. Never having experienced total darkness before, I put my hand directly in front of my face and could not see it at all. Relief came when we turned our lights back on.

I had invented the "Challenge" almost twenty years ago. The cavern the students had entered is about fifteen feet high and nearly forty feet in length. At the beginning, there is a mud bar, and the water is usually only about a foot deep. However, that changes rapidly as the cavern is actually a spring, and the bottom drops away quickly. That year, for no particular reason, I had decided to climb the walls and circumvent the entire cavern. Without saying anything, I had put my flashlight in my mouth and started to climb.

With my flashlight firmly in my mouth, I could not tell the students not to follow. They all did, and it was not long before I heard the splash and gasping as one of them lost grip and tumbled into the icy spring water. By the time I reached the end of the cavern, I was alone on the wall. The "Challenge" had been created.

Bill's Journal

A large cavern spread out before us. It was at least twenty feet wide, and our lights found its end a minimum of fifty feet in the distance. Water came to our shins, but quickly got deeper as the whole cavern was a water-filled spring. Nobody knew how deep the water was at the end, but my guess was over a hundred feet.

Victoria's Journal

Light beams reflected eerily off the water and the cave walls.

Mr. Setzler explained, "The challenge is simple. Climb the cave wall all the way to the end and back."

He continued," Put your flashlight into your mouth and follow me. By the way, remember not to try and talk or you'll lose your light," he chuckled dissonantly.

No one laughed. Crazily we followed him into the water and onto the cave wall. Soon our arm muscles burned while we clenched the cave walls moving ever so slowly towards our goal.

Kailee's Journal

It was Lindsey's fault; she was in front of me, and I forgot the no-talking warning. My flashlight plunged from my mouth and into the water. It didn't even go out, but continued to send a pillar of light up from the depths of the spring.

Victoria's Journal

I don't know who fell first, but I heard a splash and a weak gasp followed by the thrashing sound of a desperate swimmer. Other splashes followed as more of us succumbed to gravity and peeled off into the frigid spring. Cold water immersed my entire body; I had surrendered.

Only Bill, Kate, and Mr. Setzler were left. They clung sloth-like at the far end. Kate took her dip, followed shortly by Bill. Mr. Setzler valiantly attempted to stay on the wall, but in the end, he weakened and joined the rest of us. Finally, after all the screams and geysers of water, we had had enough and gathered in the relative safety of the shallow water.

Bill's Journal

Back through the dreaded drip holes, over and under the numerous cave formations, and down the waterfall, we made our way to the cave entrance. The night air was refreshingly warm and the usually cold river felt as warm as bath water. We plunged right in and swam across.

Kailee's Journal

I have no idea how I made it or how I did not get hypothermia. What I do know is that without even thinking about it, I would do it over and over and over again!

"It's so hot out here! The river is so warm!" unidentified students screeched from the cave mouth and across the river.

"The cave was awesome! I did the challenge!" the voices continued to knife through the darkness.

The first four walked into the water to "warm up!" From the other side, I explained to them how to swim at an angle into the current. One at a time they made the night swim and emerged feeling very proud and positive about themselves. Eight students used the strength of the swift river current to make the crossing. (There was a shallow gravel bar just below so there was no real danger, but I didn't tell them that.) The last two paddled across with Chris and Diane.

3rd Night

Changed into dry clothes, the students lined up along the log for supper. (It must have been 6:00 P.M. Ha!) Grabbing a plate and spoon (we don't carry forks) they first were served heaping amounts of a cheddar cheese topped salad. Mounds of macaroni and cheese were next, followed by several hot dogs which were stuffed either into bread or tortillas. Cold raspberry juice on ice completed the meal. Tina and I served, and everyone ate until stuffed.

Sitting in the dark, we realized we had lots of wood, but no fire. Diane had expressed the desire to teach her girls how to build one properly. Respecting her request, we let her begin the lesson. Birch bark first, small twigs, and soon a fire was roaring. It's radiating warmth and light was welcome in the cold dark.

Tina's girls did the dishes in the light of my small lantern. Every few minutes Chris and I would feel wet raindrops splashing across our backs. We would look up at the clear stars and then back at the four innocent faces of our "kitchen police."

"I love doing dishes out here!" laughed Kellie while sending another spray of water towards our already soaked backs.

A log erupted in a small shower of sparks. One of the random hot coals found its way up the pant leg of Lindsey's shorts. While performing a wild fire dance, the coal fell from the same side of her posterior that a rock had cut the day before. We all agreed.

Lindsey was very entertaining.

Dishes tucked under the log and food packed securely in the York packs, we settled back to enjoy the fire. I had saved squares of semi-sweet chocolate for a special occasion. With all we had accomplished today, the time was right, and they were passed out and quickly devoured. The chocolate was much better than the runny pudding of the previous night.

Out came our endless supply of marshmallows. The yapping of the seals began again while Chris tossed the waiting students their sugary rewards.

When the fire was merely a batch of glimmering coals, I told my bear stories. With darkness closing in around us, I retold the story of the Glacier Park mauling that occurred in the late sixties and several other gruesome tales. Only the river could be heard in the background while thirteen pairs of anxious eyes focused on my every word. Concluded, I said it must be nearly nine. They were gone.

Only Victoria remained, "Thanks for the stories, Mr. Rigby. Those will make it a lot easier to sleep tonight!" Sarcasm dripped from her words.

Camp set, all exhausted, Diane headed up to her tent. Chris and I headed to ours leaving Tina by the fire. The rocks were so "soft" I didn't even bother to blow up my mattress. We talked briefly about how lucky we were to have such a great group to work with. We also discussed how we had covered twenty-nine river miles in the past three days. We would have to paddle twenty-seven tomorrow. It would be a challenge. Across the river a barred owl called gently. We were soon asleep.

8/11/04 Wednesday
Third Morning

Some strange bird called from across the river. I am awake. It calls again, and I sat up looking out the front screen at the ever-flowing river. For a third time the strange bird call rings from the woods. Ok I'm up already!

There had been no need for the use of my green mattress, so I did not have to deflate it. Silently, without disturbing Chris, I slipped out of the tent and into the chill on the yet sunless morning. Diane was brushing her waist long hair next to the river. We nodded, smiled, and exchanged a silent morning greeting. The early morning river casts a peaceful spell that must remain unbroken and enjoyed for as long as possible.

After lighting one of the Coleman stoves and placing a small pot of water to boil, I splashed cold river water on my face and torso. The icy water bites into my skin and sharpens my senses. By the time I am dried, the water is boiling. Diane chose hot chocolate, and with my coffee in hand, I retreat to a secluded spot at the root end of our fallen tree table. Sandal-clad feet immersed in the water, I slowly loosen joints and stretch stiff old muscles practicing my Tai Chi routine. Today, looking across the river where the tops of the trees are just starting to turn golden from the awakening sun, the routine is especially pleasurable!

Sometimes it takes a couple of days for my body to adjust to living in the out-of-doors. I have adjusted and feel a warm glow of peacefulness that only the early morning tranquility of a wilderness setting can produce. Sipping my coffee, I sat on our log and opened the Bible I carry on all trips. Reverend Cecil C. Urch presented this cherished book to me in April of 1963. It has been my wilderness companion since. I read a passage from Luke, then the 23rd Psalm. "He leads me besides still water; he restores my soul." Yes he does!

Caity has joined Diane. She flashed her ever-present smile and senses the quiet mood of the river. She does not disturb it. I settled into my journal. We have a hard day ahead; twenty-seven miles of river need to be paddled. We have covered less than twenty-nine miles in the last two and a half days!

Diane joins me on the log. "Can I drag the kids out of their tents and throw them in the water?" she asks.

I know she would love to.

"How about just waking them gently; we don't want to disturb our neighbors," I answered, saving them from a dunking.

"Ok, you're right," she smiled nefariously.

With her wicked grin still in place, she moved towards the first tent. The silent, tranquil mood is broken; Diane is right. We need to get on the river. Students stumbled out and snarf up bagels, hot chocolate, oatmeal, granola, and Tang. I joined Chris at our tent. He thanked me for the extra sleep.

Our tent is soon down and stuffed into our granite gear compression sacks. Kate comes over to make our daily switch of the sleeping bags. Even with the compression sack, her bag is too big to be packed in the bulkhead of her kayak. She carries mine away. We trust each other completely to keep each other's sleeping bags dry.

Tina's girls set out to do the BMI study. I asked Diane to help, and at first Tina protested. Then she realized that Diane really has the expertise to help her and her girls learn, so she welcomes Diane's company.

Tina had been an aid at our school and loved helping the science staff. She sleeps by the fire, fighting off nightly raccoon attacks. She is a woman who possesses a never-ending supply of energy. She provides the much appreciated warmth of a mother when the need arises. She is a tremendous asset to the trip.

With Chris and the boys packing away the last of the breakfast dishes, I joined the BMI study. I asked Diane to test one more area. One mean scowl, then a nod of approval. She and Tina lead the girls to a different riffle area to collect.

Again our results are the same even though the critters are slightly different. The river rates a consistent very-good. These results will truly be valuable for comparison in the spring.

Canoes packed, the students gathered at our kitchen log one last time. I read from my journal what I had written in the quiet tranquility of the pre-dawn.

Mr. Rigby's Journal

It is early, it is quiet, yet really it is not. The river murmurs its constant melodic song, rhythmically flowing over the many different brown rocks. To my right, the water slams gently into the roots of the fallen tree that has made our table. Low gurgles immerse from the log, the bass of the river choir.

Diane was up fishing when I arose, and we shared hot drinks to the harmony of the river's ensemble. Tina is actually asleep, curled by her now gray-ashen fire. Chris gets up. Finally, I had been able to get out of the tent without waking him. A cricket nymph lands on my pant leg, but leaps away when I bend to observe him more closely.

Caity is the first student up, and she sits quietly talking with Diane. Soon others will rise, and the river choir will be drowned out as the camp comes to life.

Cliffs today. I hope it is sunny and warm or warm or sunny. This is what Kailee has been really looking forward to. Will she make the day without getting hooked again? Will Lindsey be able to not lose anything to the phantom Marmagauysey who keep stealing her stuff? Will Kate keep her gear dry? Will Kellie stay upright? Will Alexis continue to pound Caity with water? Will Caity learn how to splash? Will Ricky catch a fish? Will Bill ever run.out of interesting facts? Will Victoria smile in the morning? Will Lil Jemima cast a spell or throw a fit?

"It's a gift to be simple
It's a gift to be free.
It's a gift to come round
Where we ought to be."
"Old Shaker Hymn"

We have a special challenge today. We need to cover twenty-seven miles of river. Let's get to it!

Reading done, we returned to our canoes where Kailee and Lindsey are ready to go. "Thank you, campsite!" I whispered quietly while giving a fisted salute. This had been a really special site. We exchanged greeting with our new found friends from Illinois and set out for our twenty-seven miles of paddling.

Morning Paddle

Lindsey and Kailee are excellent canoe mates. We talked about many things while we paddled. However, today Kailee unintentionally hammered me. First, we somehow are talking about movies, and I brought up my favorite actor, Clint Eastwood.

Kailee said "Who? He must be really old."

I scoffed at the age referral, and she tries to make me feel better by stating, "I'll bet my grandpa knows him; he's 67."

"Thanks. Now your saying I act like I'm 67!" was my retort.

Trying to redeem herself she continues, "My gramma is 53 just like you, but she died."

"Did you know the average male life expectancy is 86?" chips in the now sterning Bill, with another of his never-ending facts of trivia.

Sometimes it's hard for me to realize that I am forty years older than the students. Then again, there is always someone like Kailee to set me straight. We pulled our canoes into Carr's landing to get ice and supplies for s'mores.

Before getting out, I innocently ask Lindsey why one girl's tent had smelt so much like swamp gas last night.

"It was her!!!!! "

Without hesitation all the girls pointed at the now face-buried-in-her-lap Kailee. Revenge is sweet!

The girls sprinted towards the cement washrooms. From inside, I could hear delighted screams.

"Mirrors! Real mirrors!"

"Warm water!"

Finally an exclamation of, "They flush! They actually flush!"

Re-supplied, we paddled under the Rt. 19 Bridge. It is one of only two bridges we traversed in our fifty-six mile paddle. Two miles down and only twenty-five to go. Clouds have blocked the sun, and the temperature has dropped. It is a perfect day to cover ground!

We dug in with our paddles, but we do not fly down the river. We are slow. We talk, tell stories, and river miles pass by methodically. This is an easy section of river, but it is also less interesting. Chris and Diane both have low-grade headaches and Tina's shoulder is very sore. I can feel the spirit of the group beginning to sag. Diane says it's the new low pressure area bringing in the cold and clouds that is doing it. I think we need to sing.

I sang two songs quietly to get myself warmed up and hear short quips of others singing individual tunes. The river is wide and we bunch all the canoes together forming a large floating barge.

As a young college student, I had captained the University of Illinois Rugby Team to the Big Ten Championship in 1972; because of rugby traditions, I know plenty of songs. The problem is that none of them are appropriate for students or really anybody. For years, however, I have sung the English Rugby version of "Aloutte." Kailee and Lindsey were anxious to sing. Along with Victoria, Alexis, and Lil Jemima, I began. Working from the head downward, they laughed at the verses which included dirty hair, smiled at the blood-shot eyes and roared while singing about her snotty nose. Kailee had no clue what a stubbly chin was, but laughed anyway.

Then the verse got personal for a thirteen year young female.

Thinking back, I could still picture our long since retired Superintendent in the late seventies, standing in the back of his canoe proudly proclaiming with both hands demonstrating "her droooooooping br........"

It was cold, drizzly and we had miles to go. This group needed something "different" to spur them on. I went for it. I was solo. They giggled, blushed and looked doubtfully at each other. Chris was laughing so hard he almost fell from the back of his canoe. There was only one more verse I could sing, and our effort was feeble at best.

Victoria asked, "Can we do it again? We'll do better!" she promised.

They all nodded in agreement.

The river valley rang with the now vibrating verses. Like a troop of true French Voyageurs, our canoes sped down the river, canoe stokes in time with our ridiculous song. "Aloutte" was followed by "Hole in the Bottom of the Sea" and then the "Music Man." Time and miles flew by, and soon we were nearing the cliffs of our jump site and lunch.

Knowing the lunch site was a very popular campsite and would be picked clean of fire wood, we made a stop at a gravel bar to load up with wood. It was cold enough that we would need a fire to be able to enjoy our lunch. Bill and I broke down a twenty-foot dead "widow maker" tree, and soon all canoe bow areas were filled to the brim with dry dead wood.

The stream on the river left that marked the beginning of the high cliff area was almost dry. The small gravel bar that had been just large enough for one tent had quadrupled in size. I needed to remember that for future trips.

Dolomite cliffs rose over a hundred feet straight from the river. The current turned and ran straight at them along the base of the magnificent multicolored rock face. Our canoe headed directly at the rock and wham--we smashed hard against it. We lurched, but remained upright. Whoops! My Bad!

We drifted swiftly along the cliff base on the deep aqua water. The bottom was nowhere to be seen. Strong eddies cradled our craft into the shallows. We beached on the flat gravel that spread from the river's edge to the trees over thirty yards away. No sun was present to argue or dispute our appetites which proclaimed the time as noon--lunch.

3rd Lunch

Diane's group was "cooks" for the day. With the precision of a well-practiced drill team, they carried York packs and supplies to a gravel ridge and started lunch. Tina's group was unloading fire wood and carrying it to the spot she had selected for the fire. I took a cast and caught a small fish. Handing my pole to Ricky, I let him continue his fishless efforts further down the shore.

Chris and Bill came over and started helping me set up the underwater camera. With the battery hooked up, view shield set, and contrast adjusted, we launched back out towards the deep waters at the base of the cliffs. From the middle or duff section of the canoe, Bill monitored the screen. Chris held the camera and one hundred feet of cable in the bow. I directed the canoe from the stern.

We floated out under the twenty-foot ledge that has always been our favorite jump site. Chris lowered the camera while Bill watched the screen. Big rocks appeared at a depth of only six feet. The river was low. This cliff was not safe. We continued our search moving upstream along the rising cliffs.

"Look at the size of those fish!" exclaimed Bill.

Curious fish swam up to the camera, dazzled by the lights. All three of us were mesmerized by the eerie pictures of the rock strewn bottom. Twenty-feet up to the top of this vertical wall and way past twenty-feet of cord to reach the bottom. This cliff would be safe, but the weather was cold, grey, and windy.

"Lunch is ready!" came a cry from the Diane's girls.

We pulled up the camera and lowered the Secchi Disk to measure the water's turbidity (clarity.)

"Come here, Ricky. We need your arm again."

I had neglected to bring a meter stick, so we marked the depth on the rope. Since we had used Ricky's elbow for our cubit measurements at the first site, we kept the mark and paddled to shore to use him again. The turbidity measured sixteen Ricky-cubits which we recorded. We would get the real metric version upon our return to school.

We rushed over to the disappearing lunch and joined the girls at the roaring campfire. The warmth of Tina's fire was much welcomed, and we huddled close to absorb its heat. Diane ran the horse-n-goggle for the left-overs. Even though I wasn't hungry, I joined in the game. The competition was fun, and I even came away with a sand-covered piece of cheese!

I started to lay down for a quick nap, when I was disturbed by Lindsey's declaring, "We've decided to call our team the Mighty Belugas!"

"You boys are going down!" shouted Kailee while wagging her finger at Mr. Setzler.

It was time for our highly anticipated game of home run derby. No napping now!

Home Run Derby

Mr. Rigby's Journal

Chris's unnamed team of Bill, Ricky, and Chris versus our team, the Mighty Belugas! Lindsey, Kailee, and I were ready. This was the perfect location. A small peninsula of gravel protruded out into the quiet waters of the eddy pool forming the batter's box. The quick moving river stretched some forty feet to the sheer one hundred foot wall of the cliff. All the non-competing girls sat on the bank behind the batter's box to form the cheering peanut gallery.

We Belugas took our now practice-worn bat we had carved on the first day and established our place at the river's edge. Rules were clarified. One point was rewarded for each rock that cleared the river and struck the cliff. Four points (grand slam) was awarded for each rock that cleared the river and made the scruffy cedars above the rock. An out was given for each swing that did not produce a point. Three outs per team per inning, nine inning of play. This was a game for honor and pride. One fat old man and two girls versus a young, well-tuned athlete and two boys. The long-awaited competition began.

Kailee, Lindsey, and I kept a running flow of chatter to the boys offering them tips in technique and challenging their manhood.

Bill, Ricky, and Chris each swung and missed. The first half inning was complete. We did the same; it was 0 to 0. Top of the second and all three boys repeated their first inning performance and kept their score at nil. I stepped up and crushed a liner that splattered against the tall cliff. 1-0. Lindsey and Kailee both missed. Bam! I sent another rock searing against the cliff. The rousing cheers from the peanut gallery echoed along the river.

We now had a name for the boy; the Wiffin Willies.

Bill emphatically stated, "Calling us the Wiffin Willies is a distraction!"

We agreed and started chanting, "Wiffin Willies! Wiffin Willies!"

There was a short delay in the game while a group of canoers passed. They looked at us with a strange expression, not having a clue what we were doing.

Chris and I continued to exchange homers. Ricky swung so hard he spun and fell into the river. The innings passed.

Crack! Lindsey connected and smashed a rock into the cliff. The girls went crazy. Bam! Kailee powdered a rocket across the river. Wham! Lindsey hit another. The score was 10 to 4.

I bent to look for the perfect rock, then straightened when I heard the boys shouting, "Grand Slam! Grand Slam!" Chris had just powered a rock up and into the towering cedars at the top of the cliff. 10 to 8, bottom of the eighth inning. All three of us Belugas choked, and it was the ninth.

Last chance for the Wiffin Willies. Amidst jeers and catcalls, both Bill and Ricky swung so hard they twisted into the water producing nothing but wind.

Up stepped the Mighty Setzler. A home run would prolong the game; a grad slam would propel them into the lead. Chris dug in his feet, looked at the cliff, and tossed his rock.

For years we have played this simple game. Students have raced through their camp chores to grab a stick and stand swinging at the shore. All three of my sons had been seasoned veterans.

Chris's rock floated upwards. He squinted his eyes in concentration, the only sound the rushing water. With all his might he swung! He missed! The Mighty Setzler had struck out. Cheers reverberated off the cliffs as we Belugas exchanged high fives. Hand shakes and condolences shared, we loaded the canoes.

Just as we were about to push off, Lil Jemima strutted up to our canoe. "You Belugas are going down! We challenge you to another game!" Hands on hips, fingers wagging defiantly, Diane and her girls laid down the gauntlet.

Because rain threatened and we had miles yet to paddle to get to Twin Rocks, the game would have to wait.

Afternoon Paddle

I felt bad that we could not cliff jump. Kailee and many of the group really had looked forward to this. It was just too cold and with the treat of rain, not wise. We paddled on.

I started trolling with an orange rapalla and soon hooked a small mouth bass. I handed the pole to Lindsey but I had not set the hook adequately. The fish got loose. The girls were hooked, however, and they took turns casting and holding the pole while we trolled.

Lindsey had her journal out and was writing with her right hand, the pole in her left. We teased that she was trying to "fool" the fish into thinking she wasn't paying attention. The pole lurched, and she fought a small mouth to the edge of the canoe. I quickly released it and it was

Kailee's turn. She got snagged and handed the pole back to Lindsey. Shortly after picking up her pencil to write, another small mouth struck her lure. She caught and released two more fish in this manner while our canoe passed under the towering 200-foot-plus cliffs of Bee Bluff and through the deep strong eddies of Jecktail Landing.

We rejoined the rest of the group where they had beached their canoes on the gravel bar across from Twin Rocks. Twin Rocks consists of three humongous cube-shaped rocks that fell away from the sheer cliff behind them some time in the distant past. The flat surface at their top forms a platform over fifteen feet above the water's surface. This was the students' last chance to cliff jump. The clouds seemed higher and there was even a small patch of blue moving in our direction.

"What do you think, Kailee?" I inquired.

"Yes! Let's do it!" she exclaimed, her eyes wild with excitement.

"Darn!" I thought. "Don't they know how cold it is?"

Diane quickly volunteer to fish and walked off down the gravel bar with her pole. Chris just shook his head and paddled his canoe out into the current to act as a life guard.

"No way, it's too cold," his eyes sent a clear message to me. I peeled off my shirt and dove into the water. "Oh, God, this is sooooo cold!" my body screamed. "Why?"

"Cliffs, jumping from high places, that is what I'm looking forward to. I love the adrenaline rush and can't wait" Kailee had said that first night by the fire.

Of course we had to jump!

From past year's experience, we knew the depth approached nearly thirty feet, but we always checked for new obstacles. One dive convinced me it was plenty deep; I could not find the bottom.

The exuberant students were soon thrashing across the water in their life jackets. A low ledge of rock protruded out between the two highest rocks. I pulled myself up and stood on the ledge shivering and covered with goose bumps. They didn't seem to notice the cold as I helped each one up and onto the rocks. All were soon clamoring up the sheer dolomite face. Without hesitation, like lemmings on a death march, they were throwing their bodies off the top and into the cold water. I stood shaking on the ledge, delighted that they could experience at least one of the jump sites. The students could have continued jumping for hours, but the sun kept getting lower.

"Last jump!" I announced. "We still have lots of river to cover!"

One more jump each, and they swam back across to the gravel bar and the waiting canoes. I was too cold to get in the water again. I let Chris pick me up, and we ferried the canoe back to the group.

On the river I could sense the group was getting tired. I began to entertain thoughts of pulling in short of our destination and getting up early tomorrow to finish the trip. No! We had set a goal, and as long as it was safe, we "needed" to strive to achieve that goal. We pressed on.

Alexis and Kellie switched handling the stern in the student canoe. Despite her slender build, Lindsey had proven to be an exceptionally strong paddler. We moved her in with Kellie and Alexis to provide more power.

Kailee and I were now alone in our canoe. She liked to take one paddle then sit and watch or talk. That was ok; she had worked hard and was getting tired.

The three girls raced down the river. Somehow, with their new found speed, they did not notice a root wad sticking three feet out of the water. It was in the exact middle of the river in plain view. They hit it full speed, head on. Their canoe flew up on top and came to an abrupt halt.

"Where'd that come from?" exclaimed a surprised Alexis.

We all sat laughing, marveling at how they could hit something so big, so perfectly, yet they somehow had stayed upright. In fact, they were wedged so tightly that it took several minutes for them to free themselves.

Our group passed Two Rivers Landing and the little store with the great root beer. We didn't really need anything, and the sun was now below the trees.

"Let's keep going," I stated.

Diane nodded agreement and then led her group in singing, "There's a hole in the bottom of our boat! There's a hole in the bottom of our boat! There's a hole. There's a hole. There's a hole in the bottom of our boat!"

Abby bailed for effect.

We floated briskly through a shoot by a campsite we have used regularly on the last night. It was occupied.

With Diane's crew still singing and the sun just dipping out of sight, we rounded another bend to the campsite we had found last year. It was open. We beached in the gravel at the base of a five-foot ledge that led to the sprawling gravel of our spacious home for our last night on the river.

4th (Last) Camp

It must have been the adrenalin rush of achieving our goal. Twenty-seven miles is a long way. We had done it!

Exhausted muscles were forgotten, and in the growing darkness, canoes were hauled up the shore and turned into tables. Unlike the first night where the students needed direction for everything and chaos was the rule, now everyone pitched in and jobs were completed quickly and efficiently. I found a honey hole of wood; Bill and Ricky found another. Tina sorted and we collected an awesome supply in no time at all. Dry clothes, long pants, and wind breakers on; we looked up to see the sky clearing. It would be a starry, cold summer's night. It was August and we would also be entertained by a meteor shower. Spirits soared even higher.

Diane and I met at our canoe table to discuss supper. Pizza, this was a gamble. I had listened to a guide (Cliff Jacobson) explain how to cook pizza on a trip. I tried it at home, perfected it on solo trips, and then tried it on my brothers a few weeks ago in Canada. Now we were going to try and prepare pizza for fourteen very hungry people who had just paddled twenty-seven miles. Plus, it was dark. Nothing like another challenge!

"Here's the veggies," stated Tina.

Stored in the coolness of her kayak's bulkhead, green peppers, mushrooms, tomatoes and onions had stayed fresh for the entire trip. Diane had her girls start grating cheese and cutting the veggies. They also started on the large salad. Chris thankfully volunteered his help, and we set up two Coleman stoves on the opposite side of the canoes, away from the fire. I sat comfortably on my stool, and Chris pulled up the cooler.

"Could you use some light, Mr. Rigby?" Bill asked.

"I'll help with the pitas." added Ricky.

The two stood beside Chris and I, providing us with light from their flashlights while handing us pitas. Soon we had pitas browning in fresh seasoned olive oil. Chris continued working on browning all eighteen pitas while I fried hard salami, mushrooms, and the rest of the veggies.

"Man that smells good! I'm starved!" exclaimed Chris.

The aroma multiplied our hunger. All fourteen of our group was now totally immersed in creating a final feast.

With the ingredients prepared, the students lined up and each took a browned pita. After spreading pizza sauce on the pita, they sprinkled it with oregano and garlic. Veggies and hard salami were next. Topped with mounds of mozzarella cheese and sprinkled with cheddar, they then brought their concoctions to Chris and me for the final stage.

"Please!" was all Lil Jemima said while holding her plate out for me to take.

We slid her pizza back into the frying pan with the searing hot olive oil. We than added a dash of water and covered it. Through the clear glass of my frying pan lid, Lil Jemima and I watched the cheese quickly melt and spread to cover her entire masterpiece. Sliding her creation back onto her plate, she smiled and headed off to the fire to gorge.

"Yummmm! That looks good. Thanks."

Chris and I made twelve pizzas before cooking our own. Leaving ours to cool at our feet, we prepared the last four to be split for seconds.

"Darn, I can't believe I did that!" declared a disgusted Bill.

A testament to how good the pizzas were was accidentally made by Ricky and Bill. While carrying their second pizza to the fire, it slid off their plate onto the gravel. Without uttering a word, they meticulously set about picking every piece of stone out of their treasure. Then they gobbled down their pizza in satisfied silence. Only the crackling of the fire could be heard. All of us sat stuffing ourselves until we could eat no more. At least for that moment, our students always recovered their appetites quickly.

Tina's roaring fire provided the light for Chris and the boys to clean the dishes. Meticulously, they washed and packed away the multitude of dishes. They would accept no help.

"Whoever is sleeping out by the fire needs to get their bags now!" declared Tina.

The students scrambled to their tents and all brought out their sleeping bags to join her in sleeping under the stars for the final night.

Under the Stars

Alexis' Journal

"Forget the tent!" We girls exclaimed. We were given the option of sleeping out next to the fire, and we were going to take it.

An extra-large pile of fire wood had been gathered. The wood from several "honey holes" was piled high. We even had constructed a wooden bench for everyone to use. Ricky and Bill had come back to camp saying they had a log that would take five people to carry. They were right! We added it to our night's supply.

Dishes done, we all grabbed our sleeping bags and nestled in the rocks next to our blazing fire. Everyone, Tina and even Ms. Dorn had their sleeping stuff by the fire. Everyone, that is, except for Mr. Rigby and Mr. Setzler. They said they needed a good night's sleep for the long drive coming up tomorrow. Mr. Rigby and Ricky got out the s'more kit of chocolate and graham crackers. Mr. Setzler tossed us marshmallows. We sat talking about all we had done on the trip and then about home. We all shared things we missed and looked forward to doing when we got home. Yet, we did not want the trip to end.

Down to our last piece of chocolate, we decided to horse n' goggle for it when Caity said, "I don't need chocolate. What do ya think? It isn't making ya skinny!"

I don't know why, maybe too much sugar, but I thought that was the funniest thing I had ever heard. My mouth was stuffed with chocolate, marshmallow, and graham crackers. So when I started to laugh, I began to choke, cough, and drool all at the same time.

"You're drooling chocolate, Alexis!" exclaimed Kate.

Everyone was laughing at me. I kept trying to explain what Caity had said but couldn't. Chocolate drool gushed from the corners of my mouth, and I could not stop laughing.

Kate's Journal

Settled, the fire turned to mostly coals while we laid back in our bags and watched the stars. Constellations like Cassiopeia, the Dippers, and the Northern Triangle were pointed out by Ms. Dorn. An occasional meteor streaked across the sky. It was August, and we were treated to a meteor shower. We lay there in silence, disturbed only by the quiet murmurs from the river, counting the blazing falling stars. Late into the night we just stared in wonder until sleep began to take us one at a time. Tina was still adding wood to the warm fire when I finally drifted off, but not before I had counted twenty-six meteors.

Contently full, exhausted, sore, but completely exhilarated by the outcome of the day, Chris and I were the only ones to retreat to our tents. (I don't sleep well under the stars. I keep looking.) We had a long drive and wanted to be prepared. Diane, however, brought her bag out, and for the first time since I have known her, joined the students and Tina around the fire. I fell asleep to the quiet laughter and soft conversation coming from the sleepy group by the fire.

8/12/04 Thursday
Fourth (Final) Morning

I opened my eyes to see the pink glow of pre-dawn through the back screen window and yet another beautiful sunrise. I left my bag and pad behind so as not to disturb Chris and slid through the open screen door out into the cold morning mist. A grey curling tail of smoke wound skyward from the spent fire. Twelve bodies tucked deep in their bags lay in motionless silence.

Toiletries and towel under arm, I headed over a gravel hill and downstream to prepare my body for the day. By now I was physically and psychologically adjusted to some of the rougher parts of wilderness camping and was able to comfortably "take care of business" as Victoria would say. Refreshed, cleaned, and leaving no trace, I quietly made my way back to camp to start some coffee.

Tina soon had a fire going, and heads began to pop out of the sleeping bags. With my cup of hot coffee in hand, I retreated to the river's edge for my morning ritual of Tai

Chi and Bible passages. The sun burnt the mist off the campsite quickly and warmed us all. Students stumbled over each other to get bagels and hot chocolate. Kailee tried walking in her sleeping bag but fell hard on the rocks and lay there laughing. A typical morning had begun.

Chris, Diane and I joined each other on a small gravel ridge thirty feet behind the camp fire and sat drinking our hot mixtures.

"What a show we had last night! The sky was full of meteors; it was unbelievable!" Diane was excited about all the "shooting stars" they had seen.

"We are so lucky. These kids are just the best!" Chris was excited about how wonderful the students had been and how lucky we are to have such great kids at our school.

I agreed with them both.

On the last morning, there are no assigned duties; everyone just helps each other. On some trips students need to be instructed and coaxed to complete tasks. Not this group. Without instructions, packs got packed, tents taken down and canoes loaded. Kate and I exchanged sleeping bags, Bill and Ricky helped each other pack, and Diane and the girls carried their gear towards the river.

We gathered at the river's edge, and I read one last section from my journal.

Jose's Challenge

Mr. Rigby's Journal

Jose had said to me, "I challenge you to bring back to your students a love for the earth that you feel. Live with the earth on your trip. Listen to the earth. Let the water talk to you. Listen to the birds and trees and feel what they have to say. Be one with the earth."

Well Jose, how did I do?

Did we live with the earth?

I think so. We slept on the rocks. We laid out watching the stars streak across the sky. We wore the earth as we slid through the depths of the caves and came out covered with clay.

Did the water talk to us?

It sure did! We heard the water speak to us as we lay in our tents. We felt the icy cold of the springs and the warmth when we came out of a cave. We felt the power of a rapid and the gentle stillness of a pool.

Did we listen and feel what the birds and the trees had to tell us?

The whip-poor-wills roused us at night. Soft bird calls woke us in the morning. We learned a respect for trees and how quickly they can tip a canoe, how their shade can be so welcome on a hot afternoon, or how the heat from their gift of fire can feel so good on a cold night.

Were we one with the earth?

We traveled with quiet respect and left our campsites better than we found them. We relished the warmth of the sun, the coolness of the river, the warmth of a fire, the coolness of a cave. We were one.

I hesitated. On this cool summer morning, the warm sun felt good. The water behind me gurgled quietly. We stood in silence. Then I continued.

What good is it? Did it teach us anything?
Like how hard is a gravel bar?
How far is twenty-seven miles of paddling?
How much can a stinging nettle burn?
Or
Don't mess with Diane!
And
Don't splash Mr. Setzler!
And
Maybe we learned a bit about self determination.
Or
How to deal with fear.
And
Most importantly,
A bit about ourselves!

We stood in silence listening to the morning sounds. Not a shred of paper or trash remained. Extra fire wood was stacked next to the well-drenched fire. Helping each other, we loaded into our waiting canoes and pushed off.

With one last clenched-fisted salute, I quietly whispered, "Thank you, campsite. Thank you, river." I took a deep breath, smiled, and then continued, "And thank you, Jose. Thanks for the challenge."

Our flotilla quietly, no, noisily paddled towards the gravel bar at Powder Mill and our waiting vehicles.

Printed in the United States
65779LVS00002B/433-603